Torque's Gaze

Author Marissa Ann

I0582435

Credits:

Cover Design by: Francessca PR & Designs

ASIN:

ISBN-13: 978-1-7365798-5-5

Credits

ISBN

Library of Congress Control Number:

Table of Contents

Chapter 1

Torque

Walking around the reception, I watch my brother Bear smile more than I've ever known him to do so. I'm happy for them but the whole falling in love bit isn't for me.

"Another wedding, another brother, leg shackled for life." I shake my head.

"One of these days some woman is going to come around and change your mind about love." Blade says from beside me.

"Of course you believe that, you're one of those that got leg shackled." I laugh. "Women, especially the ones that come into this club, are fucking crazy." I growl.

"Still sore about the snakes, huh?" He laughs.

"I'm still planning my revenge. I got to wait for Fiona to pop out my nephew first though. Then it is on." I vow but Blade laughs even more.

Before I can call him what I'm thinking of calling him, a tiny hand grabs my arm.

"Hey Uncle T!" I look down at Luna, Prez and Mina's little girl. She holds her arms up to me indicating she wants me to pick her up which I do and set her on the table between Blade and I.

"Shouldn't you be playing with the other kids?" I ask.

"I was trying to build a castle in the sand box but Hunter knocked it down and told me I wasn't a princess." She pokes her little lip out.

"Of course you're a princess!" I argue for her and get a cute little grin. "Come on, I'll help you build a bigger one."

Lifting her from the table, I nod at Blade as Luna and I walk towards the huge sandbox the Prez had built for the kids.

That's where I stay until the parents of the kids order them all to bed. Then I proceed to drink as much as possible, making it back to my room and passing out some time around three in the morning.

I wake to a cold nose pressed against my own. Opening one eye slightly, I'm met with a low playful growl from my dog Titan.

Titan was a street dog. I adopted him when he pissed on my buddy Austin's ex-wife. After treating him to a steak dinner, he hasn't left my side. I'm thinking about getting him his own sidecar and goggles so he can ride with me.

I don't even have to look at the clock because he wakes me up every single day at the same time, exactly like today since I took him off the streets.

"One of these days you're going to sleep in and I'm going to wake your ass up." I murmur to him.

He sits back on his haunches, tilting his head to look at me. When I close my eyes for longer than he likes, he yips right in my ear.

"Fine! I'm getting up!" I rise up on the bed just as he jumps around in circles, moving closer to the door.

Putting my clothes on quickly, as well as my boots, I grab my shades from the night stand, slipping them on before grabbing his leash.

"Let's go see if Bella's Brew has those muffins we like so much." I say, opening the door. He barks back in answer, more than ready for breakfast.

We take my jeep into town, parking right in front of the door. You can smell the coffee and other baked goods from outside.

Walking in with Titan at my side, more than a couple of the people inside, move around us, not wanting to get close.

I guess Titan does look more than a little scary. He's a huge ass dog with a wide head that's a credit to his breed. But it's also that breed that everyone is so afraid of without even having a reason to be so. Kind of the way most are afraid of bikers.

We get in line behind everyone else waiting to place their order. I'm looking towards the back, hoping to get Bella's attention when someone runs into my back.

"Oh, I'm sorry. Excuse me." I hear a very feminine voice.

"That's okay." I answer automatically.

Looking at the woman, I'm shocked at how beautiful she is. Her heart shaped face looks up to me for only a minute before looking down at Titan who has pushed his whole face into her midsection.

"Hello handsome guy." Her voice didn't have sweetness in it for me. Hell, she's actually barely acknowledged me. This never happens. Women always turn back for another look, even with my shades on.

She's not the classic beauty that I see so many men chase after. She's short, her head barely coming to my chest with rich dark hair, dark eyes and plenty of meat on her bones.

I really love those kinds of women. The ones that I don't feel as though I'll break if I put my arms around them.

Still not looking at me with any interest at all, she smiles slightly in my direction before walking out the door.

"Oh, did you meet the new veterinarian? She's such a sweet woman." Bella must have come up next to me when I was distracted.

"That's the new town vet?" I ask, looking back at the door.

"Yep. You'll probably see her a good bit over at Hayden's place for a while. They are still trying to find what's making the horses sick. Here, I saw the two of you out here, figured I'd bring you the usual. We are super busy this morning." Bella says in a rush.

"Thanks." I reply. "Think I'll take this to the park and let Titan play for a bit while we eat." I say.

Leaving Bella's Brew, I think back on the beautiful Veterinarian. I hope I do get to see more of her. With a smile, I enjoy my breakfast just a little more than usual.

Jesse

Sitting at my desk, I read through every page the state agricultural lab sent back on all the samples that I collected from Wolf's Landing, the Dude ranch owned by the local motorcycle club.

When I first opened my new veterinarian clinic in town, I wondered about the guys in leather that I would see riding their bikes.

None of the townspeople seemed the least bit concerned with them which helped to put my mind at ease. Where I'm from, men on bikes and dressed in leather should be avoided at all costs.

It seems that their club is very welcome in this town although when I did some digging on the internet about them, not everything that popped up was pleasant to read.

I met their Vice President, Blade, first at the local coffee shop. Since then, I've met quite a few more while working out at the ranch for Hayden. Several of her horses have gotten sick from some type of toxin that I've yet to find after testing nearly every plant and water source on the property.

Whatever the toxin is, it's gone from their bodies quickly without a trace. That in itself has me worried that someone may actually be injecting the horses directly with something.

From what Hayden has told me though, the only ones working out there are directly connected to the Club.

She's adamant that it wouldn't be one of the brothers. I'll take her word for it. I certainly don't want to point fingers. Several of them look as though they could easily bury me alive and sleep like a baby that same night.

"Did they find anything?" Remy, my assistant, asks, walking in behind me.

"Nothing." I sigh, tossing the papers down.

"What now?" She asks.

"Now? Now we wait. I asked Hayden to keep the horses in the pastures they have been in. Hopefully we can figure out which pasture is being targeted." I answer.

"So we're waiting for another horse to get sick?" She asks with concern.

Shaking my head, "Yeah. It sucks but at this point it's all we can do. I'll still go out there and take a look around every chance I get. I'd rather not watch another horse die like that."

"Me either." She answers softly. Hearing the bell above the door, she heads back towards the reception desk.

Grabbing my lab coat, I get ready to see my next patient who's coming in to get her stitches out after having her leg amputated.

Three legged cats can do everything a four legged one can. Hopefully, this time, she stays away from the highway if she gets out again.

My feet are killing me a few hours later as I walk around the clinic locking up. My stomach rumbles reminding me that I skipped lunch again today.

I've still not gone to the grocery store and decide that I'm not going to tonight either. It's just easier to pick something up from Bella's Brew.

Of course my sister, Annie, wouldn't approve. She thinks I need to be on a diet. According to her, I'm overweight.

And what if I am? I like my curves exactly where they are. It's better than looking like the stick my sister resembles.

My phone rings as soon as I get to my car. Figures it would be her as if I conjured her with my thoughts.

Getting into the car, I let the phone connect before answering.

"What took you so long?" She demands before I can even say hello.

"I'm just now getting into my car." I roll my eyes. "What's up?"

"We went to the same school; can you at least try to speak properly?" She huffs. "Mom would be so disappointed to hear you right now."

"Good thing you're not mom then." I smile towards the phone.

"She says you're not answering her calls."

"I've just been busy. Besides, she just wants to berate me for starting my practice way out here in the sticks as she put it."

"Well she does have a point Jesse. You could make so much more money here in the city."

"That's not what I wanted. All of you knew that the whole time I was in school. I told you both multiple times I was finding a rural town to start up in. One where I could work with farm animals as well as house pets. You both should be happy for me." I roll my eyes.

Remembering that I have a candy bar in my center console, I dig it out. She must hear the paper as I tear it open.

"Not sticking to your diet then?" She asks.

"I don't need to be on a diet. Besides, I missed lunch today."

I hear her sigh through the phone gearing up for the argument that always ensues.

"You're never going to catch a good man if you don't take better care of yourself."

"First of all sis, I don't need a man when I have a vibrator that doesn't talk back unless I flip his switch. Second, I can take care of myself. Now, I've gotta go find something for dinner and head home."

"God, you are so crude!" She sighs again. "I still love you though." She says quietly after a short pause.

I stare at the phone and wonder what has gotten into her. She rarely tells me that.

"I love you too. Are you okay?"

"I've never been better. Go home, get some rest. We'll talk later." She hangs up quickly.

Shaking my head, I put the car in gear and pull out of the parking lot. She wouldn't tell me if anything is wrong anyway. She'd be afraid of me saying I told you so regardless of what it is.

I think she's wrong about me never finding someone though. One day there will be a man that will love me just the way I am. All my extra curves included.

Bulging muscles and tattoos would be a plus for him. I can just see my mother's face when seeing one of her daughters with such a man. That would be the highlight of my life.

A few minutes later the smell of Bella's Brew takes over my senses as soon as I walk through the door causing my stomach to rumble with happiness.

"Hey Jesse! Have a good day at work?" Bella asks as soon as she sees me.

"Let's just say it was a long day. My feet are killing me and I'm starving!" I smile, taking a seat at the counter.

"You've come to the right place. Do you need a menu or do you want the special of the day?" She points to the sign.

Lasagna is the special and already has my mouth watering at the thought.

"The special will be just fine."

"Coming right up!" She smiles but turns towards the door opening up.

Her smile widens even more as she watches her husband walk through. The love they hold for one another is clear for all to see with how they look at each other.

"Evening Miss Jesse." Blade smiles my way once he lets go of his wife.

"Good evening." It tickles me with how well mannered he always is with me. It just doesn't seem to fit him if you judge by the leather he wears.

My food arrives soon and I tackle it like a woman that hasn't eaten in months. I can't help it. I love food, especially food that takes over all your senses the way Bella's does.

"Good wasn't it?" I hear Blade from beside me.

"I'm sorry. I missed lunch today." I feel my face flame with embarrassment.

Throwing his hands up, "Hey, I'm not judging. I eat it the same way!" He points down at his empty plate.

"What does she put in her food anyway? I swear it's become my drug of choice since moving here." I laugh.

"It's a secret recipe. As they all are." Bella answers, walking up to the counter.

"You certainly found your calling." Gathering up my purse, I begin to dig out my wallet to pay my bill before heading home.

"We're having a cookout out at the Wolfsbane Clubhouse Saturday. You should come." Bella says.

"Aren't those for club members?" I raise my brows.

"Not this one. We have one a month out there that the entire town is invited to. Quite a few usually show up, especially the ones with kids because Mina always gets those inflatable water slides and things for the little ones to play on." Blade answers.

"Just say you'll be there. You can meet everyone else." Bella says.

"Sure. I'll be there. It's not like I have any plans anyway." I shrug with a smile.

"Awesome! We'll see you then!" Bella bounces on her heels excitedly. There's no wonder most call her a Pixie. She certainly looks like one with how tiny she is.

Getting back to my car, I head home and to my bed.

Pulling up at the clubhouse on Saturday, I can see there are a lot of people here already. Kids are running around everywhere wearing swimsuits and shooting each other with water guns.

Walking around to where everyone is at, I scan the crowd for Bella and Hayden. We all spot each other at the same time and they wave me over.

"You made it!" Bella says.

"I was beginning to wonder if I was going to be able to find a parking spot. There's a lot of people here." I laugh, taking a seat with the girls.

"I'm working on that. I've already mentioned to Timber we need to expand on the parking." Mina smiles over at me.

"Bet that went over well!" Hayden laughs.

"He informed me that if everyone would ride a bike, there would be plenty of parking and no need to expand." She shrugs.

"He does have a point." Another woman who seems to be extremely pregnant in the group says.

"Oh, Jesse this is Fiona. She's Blood's sister and also the owner of the tattoo shop, Poison Pen in town." Bella introduces us.

"When are you due?" I ask her.

"Any fucking day and I can't wait!" She sighs dramatically.

"She's currently a day over her due date." Mina says. "I've already told her she should walk around. It could help."

Fiona narrows her eyes at her. "And, I've already told you I look like a fucking whale trying to move around on land!"

They all start arguing with each other about how to help Fiona go into labor soon. "You know sex can induce labor." I flippantly say while looking around. I notice the kids playing in the sandbox and spot the guy I ran into at Bella's Brew earlier in the week.

The women break out laughing when Fiona replies, "No uh, no way that's what got me in this condition."

When I first saw him I pretended that I barely noticed him when really, I felt my woman bits scream for attention. I've yet to even see his full face since he was wearing shades indoors. The same ones he's currently wearing.

He has a huge smile on his face as a beautiful little girl attempts to cover his boots in sand. I'm so busy watching them in the sandbox that I jump when a wet tongue licks my hands.

Looking down I see a beautiful huge pit bull begging for attention. The same one that was with the sexy ass biker at Bella's Brew.

"Hey beautiful boy." I smile, rubbing his ears.

"That's Titan. He belongs to Torque." Bella says from beside me.

"Torque?" I raise my brow.

"The guy you've been staring at this whole time with the sunglasses." Fiona announces loudly.

I feel my face flush red.

"Jesus, Fi. Don't embarrass her just yet. We might want to keep her around!" Mina throws a wadded up napkin at her when she just shrugs.

"She might as well get used to me now." She groans, pushing her hand to her side.

"You okay?" Hayden asks as we all scoot to the edge of our seats.

Fiona waves a hand to all of us. "Baby just kicking my side really hard."

We all sigh in relief.

Torque

I noticed her as soon as she got here. Watching as she made her way over to the other girls. The woman is sexy as sin. When I noticed a few of the guys noticing her, I felt something I don't usually feel about a woman. Jealous.

I keep my eyes on her even while playing with the kids in the sand. Mostly just to be sure no other fucker talks to her. For some reason, I've decided she is mine. For how long remains to be seen. Right now, I'd settle for just tonight.

When I notice Titan head directly for her and demand attention I hide my smile as best that I can. That's right boy, soften her up for me.

I stay away during the bar-b-que not yet wanting to go up to her. Another first for me, I normally like to get it over with. Something tells me I need to move slowly with this one.

"Seems your dog has made a new friend." Prez says taking a seat next to me at the table.

"A beautiful one too." Blood adds, taking the other seat.

"I hadn't noticed." I shrug playing it off.

"Liar!" Blood laughs. "I'm surprised you've not moved in for the kill. Could it be that this one doesn't seem to notice that you even exist?"

"I've noticed that as well." Prez agrees.

"Could you two just fuck off?"

They both laugh at that suggestion.

A few hours later when the party is winding down, I watch as she leaves saying goodbye to the girls.

Right before she heads around the building she looks back, our gazes colliding even through my shades. I grin in her direction and watch as her face turns the perfect shade of red.

I wonder if she turns that color all over.

Fuck! I gotta find out that answer. Adjusting myself, I whistle for Titan and head towards my jeep ignoring all the pussy clearly on offer. I don't want anyone else but Jesse to calm this ache. No one else will do.

Chapter 2

Jesse

I got to Wolfs Landing really early this morning. Looking around the barn area, it doesn't look like very many people are stirring this early on a Sunday.

Not letting it deter me, I walk to the tack room for a saddle. I know how to do it by myself and I also know that Hayden prefers everyone to sign in on the clipboard hanging on the wall.

Writing in which horse I'm taking out, I grab my saddle and walk to Romeo's stall. He's the most beautiful horse I've ever seen.

A solid black mustang with a white streak through his mane that Hayden says she took in as a rescue.

He and I had an instant connection the very first time I walked into the barn. Ever since then, I prefer to ride him when I come out here. Which has been weekly here lately.

While I enjoy the time spent with Romeo, I hate the reason behind it. The first several times I came out here was for pleasure riding. Then horses on the ranch started coming down sick.

The scary part is that it's always a horse in the same pasture with Romeo. Luckily, whatever the toxin is, he's stayed clear of it.

Finally when I finish tacking him up, I lead Romeo from the barn. As I'm getting up in the saddle, I think I see someone out of the corner of my eye but once I'm in the saddle looking in that direction, I don't see anyone.

Shrugging it off, I nudge my horse down the lane towards the back pastures. I want to get a few samples from the creek in the north pasture, I found last time that I was here but couldn't get to because I was out of test tubes.

Thirty minutes later, we crest over the last hill overlooking the small valley below.

"That is so beautiful." I sigh looking at the mountains in the distance. Romeo shakes his head as if in agreement.

Petting his neck, I nudge him down to the creek below. Its spring fed coming down from the mountain. I decide to take some time for myself before I collect the samples. Today is supposed to be my day off.

I lead Romeo to a shade tree and grab a blanket from the saddle bag as well as Mina's newest romance novel. I can't believe I'm friends with a best selling author.

Spreading it out, I sit back against the tree as I settle in to read and relax for a few hours. Romeo stays close by, not walking off to leave me. Thank goodness because I get completely lost in the storyline of the book.

Hours later, I wipe a tear from my eye as I read the very last line.

I have to give it to her; the woman has a way with words. Especially all her newest novels from the last couple years.

The sex scenes? Holy hell! Her scenes have gotten even better with each book she releases. Probably has something to do with that husband of hers. Not that I would ever crush on him but the man is hot. So are most of the guys in his club.

Thinking of them, my mind conjures a picture of Torque as he grinned at me last night when I was leaving the bar-b-que.

While I couldn't see his eyes because he was still wearing those sunglasses after dark, there's no mistaking that he was looking directly at me.

Just imagining his eyes with that grin has my entire body humming, begging to be touched.

I thought my poor vibrator was going to malfunction on me last night as I had to use it many times. Every time I closed my eyes, I saw him and it got me going all over again. I better buy some new batteries.

What the hell is happening to me anyway? Men don't normally get that much attention from me. Why should they when they usually ignore my existence?

However, that grin last night proves he's not ignoring me at all. He definitely noticed me. At least in that moment he did.

He probably had too much to drink. Men that good looking never pay attention to me for long.

Grabbing tubes from the saddle bag, I walk over to the water's edge.

Filling several with water samples, I move over to the vegetation getting several different samples of that as well before packing it all back into the saddle bag.

"Ready to head back sweet boy?" I ask, rubbing Romeo's nose.

Holding onto the reins, I pull them around, grabbing the saddle horn as I put one foot into the stirrup. Just as I swing my other leg over the side, Romeo rears up.

I feel myself beginning to fall and I lose my grip on the horn. The last thing I remember is thinking that this was going to hurt before I black out.

Torque

Waking up a little later than usual for me, I take Titan for a long walk before heading back to our room for a shower.

I'm just finishing getting dressed when there's a knock at my door. Knowing it's most likely one of my brothers since the yotes never get up this early, I yell out for them to enter.

"Morning shithead!" Wrench announces, plopping his ass down in the chair next to my dresser.

"Why the fuck are you here so early? That sweet wife of yours finally gets enough of your shit and tosses you out on your ass?" I grin in his direction but he just smiles back.

"Nope. She would never do that to me. She loves me dearly."

"You just still have her fooled for now. One day she'll realize that you are just a fucked up in the head biker that's not good enough for her."

"Fuck, I hope she never realizes that shit." He laughs.

"So why are you here then?" I ask, looking directly at him.

"Prez wants everyone to take turns riding the ranch. Watching for anything out of the ordinary. The horses' getting sick with this odd toxin has Hayden on edge."

Shaking my head, "Yeah I can't blame her. Word gets out about sick horses even if it isn't the ranch's fault it can have some serious impacts. They could even be shut down."

"Yeah. So I was wondering if you'd take today. I was supposed to do it but Hayden is making me go to church with her and the kids." At his admission, I start laughing uncontrollably.

"A tad bit late for her to be worried about your soul!"

"Shut up fucker! She's trying to get the kids into that expensive ass academy on the other side of town and is trying to make us look like proper upstanding citizens to the rich snobs that run the place." He rolls his eyes but I laugh even harder. "Can you switch out me or not you asshole? I'll owe you."

"Titan and I will do it. I hope like hell someone gets you on camera trying to impress the snobs. Are you going to wear a suit?" As I ask, Wrench flips me off heading out the door without another word.

I'm still laughing thinking about him at church thirty minutes later when I pull up to the barn. Almost to the door, I notice a horse heading my direction. Looking closely I see that it's missing its rider.

When he gets close enough, I grab the reins and realize that it's Romeo. The black mustang that Hayden rescued. He's not a super friendly horse so I wonder who was riding him.

Walking into the barn I put him in his stall for now with his tack still on before going over to the clipboard and looking to see who signed in this morning.

Seeing the new vets name on the board along with Romeo's I wonder where she could be. Did she get thrown? Fuck I hope not!

Grabbing the keys to one of the side-by-sides, I grab a first aid kit as well as a blanket, throwing them into the passenger seat, taking off down the lane.

Jesse put on the clipboard that she was heading to the farthest back pasture. It's a thirty minute ride by horse back but I should be able to get there in ten minutes.

She signed in at seven this morning and it's already lunch time. There's no telling how long she's been out there.

My heart is pounding hard by the time I crest the last hill and the creek comes into view. Scanning the area, I see a white shirt in the tall grass.

Putting the side by side into gear, I floor it in that direction, skidding to a halt only feet away from the beautiful vet who is clearly knocked out and bleeding from the head.

Grabbing the first aid kit, I rip open one of the pads inside, wetting it down then slowly wipe the blood from her forehead while checking her pulse.

Pushing my shades up on top of my head, I watch her eyes for any indication that she might wake up.

"Come on baby. Wake up." I whisper before getting a little louder. "Jesse! Open your eyes sweetheart!" Finally her eyes start to flutter open, staring directly back into my own.

She starts whispering and I get closer to her face. "What sweetheart?" I ask.

"Angel." She breathes out and I laugh, shaking my head.

"Nah. I'm definitely no angel." I grin and watch her guys flicker down to my lips for a long second before she starts to try to sit up.

"Careful now. You may have a concussion." I steady her with my hands on her shoulders.

She just stares back into my eyes and that's when I remember that I removed my glasses. Reaching up, I slide them back into place cutting off her gaze from my eyes.

"Come on. We need to get you to a doctor." I finally say, helping her to stand. When she wobbles on her feet, I swing her up into my arms. She never says a word, just wraps her arms around my neck.

I don't want to put her down, she lays her head against my chest and it feels like she belongs there but she needs medical attention. I hope she doesn't pick up on my hesitation, as I walk her over to the side-by-side, setting her in the passenger seat.

When I reach over, to pull her seat belt into place, I see a smudge of mud on her cheek and wipe it away with my thumb. Her eyes go to half mast at the touch and I grin, pulling back to walk around to the driver seat.

"I'll try to drive slowly. The bumps are probably going to make your head hurt. I'm sorry." I say to her with a smile. She gives me a small smile back.

At least that's progress. She's not said anything else since calling me an angel. Hopefully she's not too disappointed in finding out this angel just might be the devil.

Chapter 3

Jesse

The ride back to the ranch hurt more than the fall. I think all the ruts and rocks Torque hit on the way back has rattled my brain loose. I know he tried to avoid them but tell that to my aching head. I even had to make him stop at one point so I could puke; the motion of the buggy made me car sick.

As soon as we got back, Torque carried me to his jeep, getting me to the hospital in record time.

Dr. Ortez was waiting for us when we pulled up and I suspect that's who Torque rapidly sent a text off to as we were speeding down the highway.

I've still not spoken to Torque and have no idea why. It's as if my tongue doesn't want to work around him. Well... it doesn't want to form words. It does however want to lick every single inch of the man.

Just where in the hell did he get eyes like that anyway? He's hot enough with the sunglasses on but when you see his eyes? It creates a supernatural phenomenon of a man that really shouldn't exist.

Even with my head pounding like hell, my body still wants to climb the man like a monkey. What is wrong with me?

Hearing the door to my hospital room opening, I crack open one eye and watch as the man that fills all of my sexual fantasies walks carefully inside.

"I brought you something to drink." He whispers carefully.

"Thank you." I whisper back, taking the cup from his hand.

"Finally she speaks." His grin is too fucking sexy. "Doc said you'd probably have a headache for a while since you have a concussion."

"When can I be released?" I ask.

"He said he will only release you if you have someone to watch over you. Since I volunteered to stay with you, he's currently getting your discharge papers ready." I look at him in surprise.

"I can take care of myself."

"I'm sure you can. Under normal circumstances. But you hit your head pretty hard. Someone has to make sure you stay awake for a while longer. It might as well be me."

"Why?" Confusion clearly in my voice. Why would this sex on legs hottie want to make sure I'm alright? He must be doing it to protect the ranch. No way would someone like him be attracted to someone like me.

The grin that slowly takes over his face has me second guessing everything I just thought to myself. I can feel my body start to heat up and I swallow hard.

His hand slowly reaches to my face, fingertips sliding down my cheek back around to my chin.

"I've been wondering. Do you turn this color all over?" He whispers even more quietly.

Fuck! As soon as we get to my apartment, I need to change my panties.

The door to my room opens behind him and he drops his hand.

"Hello my dear." Dr. Ortez quietly says. "I have your discharge papers. I've already instructed Torque here to wake you up every couple of hours and what to do in case of emergencies. Of course he has my direct cell number if I need to make a house call. Just sign at the bottom here." He hands me a clipboard.

I'm not aware of how shaky I am until I try to sign my name quickly, I hand it back to him. He turns towards Torque, handing him a bottle of pills instructing him on how many I should take and when I should take them.

"Guess we are ready to go then." Torque holds his hand out to me.

Looking at it for a minute, I place my hand in his, allowing him to help me stand before sitting down into the wheelchair that is standard procedure.

Once outside, the glaring sun beats into my eyes so hard I cringe, covering my face with my hands.

"Here." I peep one eye open at the sound of his voice. I watch in fascination as he takes the sunglasses from his own eyes, sliding them into place on my own face. "It'll help." He says.

His jeep is already pulled up to the curb and he opens the passenger door for me. When he grabs my waist giving me a boost into the seat I notice how easily he lifts me.

Can I just swoon right here? A man that can lift me easily is just hot as hell!

He shuts my door, quickly getting to the driver side and getting in himself. Before putting the jeep into gear, he reaches in the glove box, getting another pair of shades and putting them on.

At his grin, I can't stop my own from spreading across my face.

Torque

"How do you know where I live?" She asks when she opens her eyes after I've turned off the ignition.

"Small town." I shrug my shoulders, not willing to tell her I made a point of finding out before we left the hospital.

Getting out of the jeep, I hurry around to her side to help her down. She grabs onto me when she is hit by a dizzy spell. I want to pull her back into my arms and carry her, but I suspect that won't go over very well now that she is more alert. So I just hold on to her as we walk towards her apartment door.

I'm thankful that it's on a lower level because she's still not completely steady on her feet.

Taking her keys from her, I let us both in walking her straight over to the couch.

"Are you hungry? I was going to call down to Bella's Brew to order that amazing potato soup she has on special today."

"You like potato soup?" She giggles.

"Not just any potato soup, I like Bella's potato soup. That woman can cook." I reaffirm but she giggles again before grabbing her head with her hands and moaning.

"Doc told me to give you these pills but only after you've had something to eat." I tap my pocket making sure they are still there.

"Potato soup does sound good." She finally answers.

"I'll go call it in. Be right back." I take my phone from my other pocket, walking just outside her front door.

Before going back in, I call Wrench to check in on Titan since I left him out at their house before rushing Jesse to the hospital. I don't think she even realized that he was there at the time.

"Thank God you finally called!" Wrench exclaims.

"Titan okay?" I say in a rush.

"Titan is fine. However, neither of us is going to be if he stays here much longer." He laughs.

"What did he do?" I rub my forehead knowing it's going to have something to do with pissing on someone.

"Hayden has this high-end client doing a retreat with her colleagues and apparently she doesn't like dogs. Titan decided that he didn't like having a woman shoo him. He pissed on her leg."

By the time he gets the last word out, he begins to laugh hysterically as if he saw it while it happened. I wish he had taped it. My dog is a legend for pissing on snooty women!

"Fucking A!" I laugh.

"Yeah, it was great. But Hayden may ship him off to the other side of the country if you don't come get him."

"Tell one of the prospects to bring him to me. I'll text you the address. I can't leave Jess alone right now."

A few minutes later I walk back inside to find Jesse stumbling down the hall.

"Hey, you shouldn't be trying to walk just yet!" I wrap my arm around her, pulling her close.

"I gotta pee!" She whispers, looking to the door closest to us.

Walking her over to it, I flip the light on for her. She cringes from the bright light but I see a dimmer switch. When I turn it down she sighs in relief.

"I'll wait out here until you're done." I nod my head, pulling the door closed behind me.

"One of the guys is going to bring my dog Titan to me if that's okay?" I say loud enough for her to hear me.

"That's not a problem." She says back quickly.

I like that she's not afraid of him like most people. Then again, she is a veterinarian and they usually are good with all animals regardless of breed.

"I'm finished now." She says, opening the door but seems to stumble again.

Instead of just offering my shoulder, I swing her up into my arms causing her to gasp.

Fuck! That sound went straight to my cock.

Walking us both back to the couch, I sit down with her still in my arms. I grin as that rosy color takes over her face once again.

I love that so fucking much that I feel my cock growing harder through my jeans.

There's no way she doesn't feel that on her ass. I'm not about to let her go though.

Jesse

Holy hell, I may not feel well right now but that's not stopping my body from reacting to the closeness of his.

We sit together, me still in his lap for quite a while, my head resting on his shoulder. I'm nearly asleep when I wake up to a knock on the door.

Torque gently moves me from his lap to the couch, walking to the door. I can see two guys standing there. One has a bag in his hand while the other hands over the leash attached to Titan's collar.

He really is a beautiful dog with a huge block head and square muzzle. I know that most people fear the breed but in my line of work I'm very aware of dog behavior. They all give clues as to whether or not they will bite. You just have to know what you are looking for.

Spotting me on the couch, the dog heads right for me but stops himself from jumping up. Instead, he lays his huge head on my lap gently and I begin to rub his ears.

Torque closes the door a few minutes later, heading to the kitchen with the bag that I assume has our food in it from Bella's Brew.

Bringing everything to the coffee table along with a couple glasses of water, he sets everything up perfectly before giving a command to Titan who immediately lies down next to the couch.

We eat nearly silently together and I can't remember the last time I was able to do that with a man that I'm alone with.

"I told you it was good." Torque says when I take my last bite. "Here, take these." He hands me the pills Dr. Ortez sent.

Torque gets up cleaning away our dishes and I stretch my legs out on the couch. I must have dozed off because I jerk my eyes open when I feel him lifting me into his arms once again.

He heads straight into my bedroom, laying me on the bed. Thinking he's just going to walk out, I roll to my side, closing my eyes. They jerk back open when the bed dips and his arms circle my waist, pulling me flush with the front of his body.

Feeling his cock once again on my backside, I wonder if it's that hard all the time. Unable to stop myself, my ass pushes into him a little more.

His arms tighten on my waist briefly before relaxing once again. One of his hands rubs small circles on my wrist and I concentrate on that. Pretty soon, I'm fast asleep, warmed by the body pressed to my own.

He wakes me several times throughout the night to check on me. Giving me water and the pain pills from the doctor.

After every time, he climbs back into the bed with me, pulling me close before we each fall asleep again.

At one point during the night, he loses his shirt and holy hell did it take me forever to go back to sleep after that.

I wanted so badly to roll over to face him and explore every single tattoo that was on display on that massive chest of his.

It had me wondering where else he was covered in tattoos. I wanted to see exactly how far down they went past the waist of his jeans.

He didn't seem the least bit phased by my closeness. His breathing evened out quickly although his grip around my waist never slackened nor did the hardness behind his fly.

I'm not sure what time it is when I wake up and Torque is no longer next to me but Titan is in his place. I laugh when the dog licks my face then lays his head on my shoulder and falls asleep.

Maybe when I feel better I can get up the courage to make a move and see what happens. Torque wouldn't be the first man to shoot me down although I think it might hurt a little more coming from him.

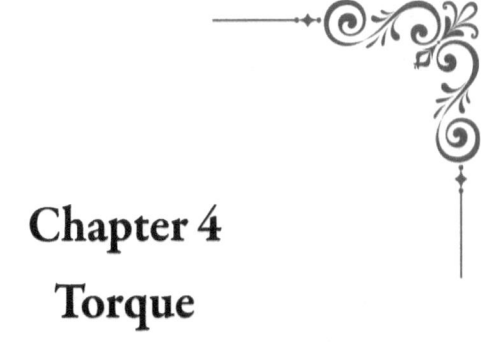

Chapter 4

Torque

Doc finally gave Jesse the all clear to go back to work today. So when she left her apartment this morning, I headed back to the clubhouse to attend Church with the club.

I couldn't stop the laugh that I barked out when Jesse thought I meant an actual Church instead of a meeting for the MC.

When I explained it to her, she turned slightly pink again and my body sprung to attention. Now all I've thought about is what excuse I can come up with that will allow me to continue to stay at her place.

It's truly surprising that I've not become bored with her yet. I even enjoy our conversations because they hold even more information about her that I find intriguing.

It's a good thing I don't hit women or her mother and sister would need to find a place to hide from me. Both of them called, leaving messages that pissed me off.

Why the fuck are they so worried about her weight for? Jesse is not overweight. She has all the right curves in all the right places that I've somewhat managed to explore while holding her close.

I wasn't a perv by any means. I certainly didn't touch her in places that I shouldn't have while she was unaware. But it was damn hard for my body to ignore her closeness and my mind went nuts thinking about all of her.

Walking into the club with Titan at my side, I spot several of the guys just standing around talking so I head in their direction.

"Finally off babysitting duty?" Fang asks.

Ignoring his question, I ask Blade, "Where's the Prez?"

"He's on his way. He had a meeting with Hawk's teacher this morning."

"What did he do this time?" I ask.

"He pushed a boy down for pulling Luna's hair."

"I can't blame him for that. He's supposed to protect his little sister." I shrug as the door behind us opens and the Prez walks in with Hawk right behind him.

"Go watch T.V. or something while I talk with the guys. If your mom asks, tell her I grounded you." He instructs and watches as Hawk runs off to the kids' room in the back.

The rest of us follow Prez into Church, taking our seats around the table.

"There's something damn odd going on out at the ranch. I'm not sure what exactly but the Veterinarian has tested pretty much everything out there and has come up with nothing. That leaves one alternative. Someone is purposely making the horses sick." Prez looks around at each of us.

"I can't come up with anyone who would still have a feud with our club. We've been legit for a long time now." Snake says.

"I hate to say it but what exactly do we know about this new vet anyway?" Fang asks.

"What the fuck is that supposed to mean?" I growl, coming halfway out of my seat. Fang holds his hands up in apology.

"Look, I'm just saying maybe she has an enemy. This shit didn't start happening until she came here and after she started coming out to the ranch for weekly rides." He explains.

"Fang is right and we still don't know what made Romeo throw her." Wrench adds.

"That horse has been unpredictable since you guys brought him in." I argue.

"True. But he acts differently with her according to Hayden. Hell, I've seen it myself. The big black beast almost purrs when she pets him."

Thinking it over in my head, I can see where his train of thought is going.

"Snake. You do all the background checks on everyone. What do you think?" Prez asks.

"I mean, sure, it's possible there's something. Nothing came up on her. I can try to do a broader sweep on the people she's connected to."

"Do that and see if you can find anything." He says just as there's a knock on the door.

Prez walks over to it, ready to cuss anyone who would disturb Church but stops short at Hawk standing there.

"I know I'm not supposed to disturb you guys but Mom made me." He says, holding a phone out to his dad.

He talks quietly for only a few minutes before getting off the phone.

"Blood? Fiona is in labor." He smiles at the room. "Church is dismissed for now. Let's go wait on our newest little member." He slaps Blood on the shoulder as he rushes to the door.

Blood and his sister Fiona are really close. They always have been and he's been really excited about becoming an Uncle to her little one.

Me too of course. But I'm also excited that I can soon get my revenge on Fiona for the fucking snakes she put in my room. It's going to be epic too!

As everyone else heads to the hospital for Fiona, I ride towards the ranch wanting to check on Romeo, the horse that Jesse loves to ride.

I leave Titan in my room at the clubhouse so that I can ride my bike. I really need to look into getting a sidecar, I hate leaving him behind. Not many of us like having to drive a cage, even one I can take the top off of.

As I'm putting the kickstand down a few minutes later at the barn, I think I see someone walking around the corner. There shouldn't be anyone here right now as Hayden made sure there was a week break between the last vacationers and the ones coming in this weekend.

When I get to the corner, I don't see anyone and figure it was just shadows from the trees close by. Going back to the barn door, I notice that the lock appears to have been pried on but it's still holding.

Looking around again for clues, I do see footprints in the sand but hell that could have been anyone. Getting the key out, I let myself in and check all the horses in the stalls.

They all still look great, even Romeo who sticks his head out looking to see what I'm doing. I stop to scratch his head and give him a treat. If he hadn't come back to the barn, who knows how long Jesse would have laid out there in the field.

I leave a few minutes later, after looking around some more and locking back up. I'll need to tell the Prez about the lock.

He's right. There's something really fucked up going on and we need to figure out what it is.

Jesse

"It feels so good to be back at work!" I stretch my arms over my head, working out the kinks still in my shoulders from my fall.

"We are all just glad you weren't hurt any worse than you were. Your sister called earlier and demanded that you call her back. I told her I would give you the message." Remy rolls her eyes, putting her purse on her shoulder.

"Thank you, Remy. I'll see you tomorrow." She waves bye before leaving out the door.

Going into my office, I gather my own things to leave and the office phone starts to ring.

"Rayne's Veterinary?" I answer quickly.

All I hear is static so I try again. "Rayne's Veterinary. Can I help you?" I say through the receiver.

"Everything you love...will die!" A deep voice finally says.

A chill runs up my back.

"Who is this?" I demand, my hand tightens on the phone.

"They will all die and so will you!" The voice whispers before I hear the line go dead.

I'm so upset that I'm shaking all over. Feeling a little lightheaded, I plop down in my desk chair staring at the phone like it's a snake that just bit me.

It has to be whoever is responsible for the animals getting sick. Any of my patients that I've spent any amount of time with have become ill. A few have even died. Luckily we've not lost any more of Hayden's horses but with that phone call I'm scared for them all.

Something has to be done and the local authorities just aren't enough. From what I've read about them and what I've heard, the club can be ruthless but at this point they are all I have. Besides, this involves them.

Grabbing my things, I lock up quickly, looking around me in all directions as I walk to my car. Pulling out of the parking lot, I gun it back towards the clubhouse hoping that I can catch Timber there.

When I pull up to the clubhouse, there appears to be a party getting started and I second guess my decision to come straight here instead of just calling first.

I'm just about to turn the car around and leave when I see Torque walking straight at me with a huge smile on his face.

Rolling my window down, I wait for him to get closer before speaking.

"Looking for me?" He leans his forearms on my door bringing his face closer to my own.

"Um, no. I was hoping to talk to Timber." Looking around once more at the crowd, I look back at him trying to see through his sunglasses. "Why do you wear those all the time?" The question just pops out of my mouth from nowhere.

"Light, any light really, hurts my eyes. I started wearing them when I was really little. It helped to keep the headaches away that I was having constantly. Not to mention the color tends to get me unwanted attention." He shrugs.

"I highly doubt the attention is unwanted. At least from the women." I grin as he grins back.

"Do they get your attention?" He whispers, moving slightly closer.

My heart rate kicks up as does my breathing and there's no way to hide the blush that crawls up my neck to my face. Stepping back, never dropping that smile of his, he opens my car door, pulling me out.

"Come on." He wraps his arm around me, leading me towards the entrance. "You said you needed to see the Prez."

"I can come back later. When you guys aren't so busy." I trail off as we walk through the door and I immediately spot a half dressed woman rubbing her breasts into the face of one of the guys.

"Fuck!" Torque grumbles when he notices where my attention went.

He pulls me closer into his side, almost pushing my face into his armpit so that I can see anything. I just hold on to him as we walk and hope I don't run into a wall or something.

He lets up slightly once we are in a hallway but never actually removes his arm from around me. Stopping at the first door he knocks once and we walk in as soon as we hear someone say enter.

"Prez, the Vet here needed to see you." Looking up, my eyes collide with Timber's.

The man always looks so fierce. I'm fairly sure that I'm a little bit afraid of him regardless of Mina being adamant that he's just a big softy.

"What can I do for you Miss Rayne?" He points to a chair in front of his desk that I sit down in immediately.

"Sorry for disturbing your party." My voice cracks and I look down at his desk.

"You're not disturbing anything. This is a celebration. Blood's sister, Fiona, gave birth to a big healthy baby boy earlier today." The look on his face when he smiles lessens the harshness.

"Congratulations. I'll have to get her something." I smile.

"Now, what can I do for you?"

"I got a really weird call just before I left work earlier that I thought you should be aware of." His brows raise but he waits for me to continue.

"The caller didn't say who they were and I didn't recognize the voice. It was a man though. He said they would all die. That everything I loved would die and so would I. " Remembering the call, my hands start to shake again.

"Go find Snake." He commands Torque who walks out immediately. "I'm glad you brought this to me. Did you call the cops?"

"No." I shake my head. "They seem to be really useless."

He laughs at my statement.

"We started to suspect that you may be the target. Torque was actually on his way to get you before you showed up here. I think for now, you should let him continue to stay at your place as a precaution." He looks right at me as if expecting me to argue but I just shake my head in agreement.

"Good." He says as the door opens again and I see Torque standing there with the man they call Snake. "Torque, take her out back to the girls. Fix her plate and get her a beer. I suspect she could use one to calm those jitters she has." He smiles warmly at me and I find myself smiling back in gratitude.

Seems Mina is right about her husband. He is a big ole softy at heart.

Snake

After leaving the Prez's office, I go grab a plate of food before heading to my computer room in the back of the clubhouse away from all the noise of the party.

I don't party much with everyone and I rarely ever bring a woman back here. If I do, it's one of the club girls that are more than okay with some ass play. On her and on me.

Some of the brothers know about my sexuality but not all of them. I don't think any of them would really give a shit though.

But after years of being treated like shit by my family for it, I'm more reserved about who knows.

Sex with just a woman still leaves me feeling empty and not just because I blew my load. I need something more. I'm just not sure I'll ever find it.

Pulling my chair up to the computer, I start the process of trying to trace the call that the vet received earlier before she left work.

I really do hate a mother fucker that likes to threaten women and animals.

They tend to be pussy's that run when confronted by someone stronger.

Cleaning my plate, I set it aside just as I hear my door open slightly. Looking over I see the Prez walking in.

"Anything?" He asks.

"Nothing. It seems to be a burner phone that leads nowhere."

He shakes his head. We both figured as much but sometimes fuckers like this tend to be a little stupid.

"Torque going to keep her close for now?" I grin.

"He seems pretty hard up for this one." I shake my head in agreement.

"I noticed but maybe she's less crazy than all the other women." He rolls his eyes at that.

"God, I fucking hope so. Maybe she can keep the others in a straighter line." He grumbles but jumps at the voice behind him.

"I doubt that but you can keep praying for it honey." Mina laughs from the door.

"I'll see you tomorrow." I wave to them both as they leave but Prez stops at the door.

"There's an envelope on my desk with the information on the crew that is supposed to be coming to help build the new cabins." He says.

"When are they supposed to be here?"

"End of the month so if you can get started on all of the background checks. I want to be sure of the guys coming before they get here." I shake my head as he closes the door behind him.

Getting up from my desk to go get the envelope, I swing my door open to see Mindy, one of the club girls, standing there in a see-through robe with a grin on her face and holding up a bottle of lube. I can't stop my own grin, pulling her into the room and shutting the door.

Jesse

After leaving the party, Torque and I head back to my apartment. Titan is riding with me in my car while Torque drives his bike.

Since they are both going to be staying with me for now, I told him that it was more than okay for Titan to go with me to the clinic every day while I work.

At first he thought it a bad idea because most people tend to be afraid of Titan. While he is right about them being scared, it's only because they don't know him and have never been around his breed before.

When we pull up to my apartment, I briefly wonder where he plans to sleep tonight. When he was here because of my concussion he claimed he had to stay in the same room to keep an eye on me.

I secretly loved every second of it. Closing my eyes, I can still feel every inch of his hard body pressed against my own. I want more of that.

"Where should I put my stuff?" Torque asks, indicating his duffel bag on his shoulder.

"In the bedroom." I answer quickly, turning to the kitchen for a glass of water. There's only one bedroom in my apartment and I hope he takes my hint.

"I'm gonna jump in the shower real quick before bed." He yells down the hall before I hear the bathroom door close.

Going to the hall closet, I get out a few blankets and an extra pillow, setting them on the couch just in case that is where he decides to sleep. Walking to my bedroom, I change into a tank top and leave my panties on before climbing between my sheets with just the bedside table on.

Laying there with my eyes closed, I hear the water shut off and Torque walk out into the hall. He seems to stand there for a few minutes before walking back towards the living room and I huff into my pillow.

I guess that is where he decided he wants to sleep tonight. I think to myself. A few minutes later though I hear him walk into my bedroom, going to the other side of the bed and climbing in.

His arms reach for me, pulling me close and my mind registers everything at once. He's in nothing but boxers and his entire body is rock hard, including the outline of his cock that is now nestled between my ass cheeks.

I feel my nipples peak inside my shirt, my core throbbing as it coats my panties with wetness. It's hard not to move against him and I'm thankful that I'm so damn tired. Otherwise, I probably wouldn't ever go to sleep tonight.

Chapter 5

Jesse

This week has been horrible! The only good I've had in my life has been the time that I've gotten to spend with Torque.

Every single night, we eat dinner together and discuss our day before going to bed where he holds me the entire night. I pray every night that he'll make a move but he doesn't and I'm too chicken to do it myself.

We get up in the morning; our routine is always the same. He follows me to the clinic where he takes a seat on the small couch in my office and stays there until I'm ready to leave. He also gets our lunch brought to us from Bella's Brew right at noon.

What's made this week so bad is the fact that a lot more patients have been rushed into my office, extremely sick. I've saved most of them but I've lost a few.

Telling a client that their beloved pet has passed is just as hard as if they were human babies. Knowing that all of this is most likely my fault makes it even worse.

There have been a few emergencies that have had me rushing to the clinic after midnight. Torque hasn't once complained, always there to help me with whatever I need. By now he should know just as much as my assistant.

Grabbing the disinfectant spray, I clean the operating table where I just lost yet another sweet dog that belonged to a little girl in town.

Her face with tears streaming down her chin will haunt my dreams forever. Just as I'm finishing the table, a cry escapes my lips that I can no longer hold back.

I'm melting to the floor when I feel strong arms picking me up, carrying me from the room. I can hear his voice rumbling but I can't make out the words through my grief.

When the tears finally stop, I realize I'm sitting in his lap on the couch in my office.

"It's not your fault you know." He whispers into my hair.

"It is though. Someone is doing this because of me."

Lifting my face up to his, he stares directly into my eyes with his own. His glasses on top of his head and I'm struck again by how beautiful his eyes are.

"That person, whoever it is, may be blaming you but you are not responsible for their actions. This shit is on them. You understand?"

Shaking my head, I just agree instead of continuing to argue. Regardless of what he says, there's blood on my hands and the truly horrible part is that I can't tell any of my clients I'm the reason their pet is dead.

"Is there anything else you need to do here before we head home?" My heart skips at him calling my apartment home.

After shaking my head no, he helps me to stand back up, taking my hand into his. Grabbing my purse, we lock up and head back to the apartment.

Soon as I'm through the door, I plop down onto the couch, toeing my shoes off. Closing my eyes, I lay my head back and must have dozed off.

I wake to Torque gently shaking my shoulder and Titan's head in my lap.

"Come on. I ran you a bubble bath. You can relax while I get our dinner ready."

At first I just stare at him like he's some kind of enigma. I've never known a man, any man, to be that considerate. At least not to me.

"You gonna stare all night or are you gonna soak that sexy ass in the bath?" He grins as I scramble to get up from the couch.

"Thank you." I grin before standing on my toes and kissing his cheek quickly.

As I turn to rush off, he spins me back around, his arms locking like bands around my body.

"Oh no. If you're gonna kiss me, do it right." He demands.

Looking right at him, I go up on my toes once more but this time, setting my lips on his. Reaching out with my tongue, I lick his bottom lip and his mouth opens over mine as he takes over the kiss.

I can't stop myself from melting into him as his tongue tangles with my own. My whole body feels like it's vibrating from the inside out.

He ends the kiss abruptly, letting go of me, a grin still on his face as I breathe heavily.

"Go relax." He says, turning me towards the hall, my body on fire with want.

On shaking legs, I make my way into the bathroom, closing the door behind me.

Torque

I wait until I hear the bathroom door shut behind her before I take a deep breath willing my cock to go down inside my jeans.

The woman has no idea what the fuck she does to me.

Finally going into the kitchen, I pull out the chicken I left to marinate in the fridge early this morning and turn the oven on.

Keeping busy helps to take my mind off the fact that she is currently completely naked just down the hall, covered in bubbles.

Glancing over at Titan, he's completely stretched out on his back on the new doggy bed that Jesse brought home for him from the clinic. He's moved over there since she is no longer on the couch for him to snuggle

Shaking my head, I go back to chopping the potatoes in front of me.

"She'll probably have your big scary ass in a tutu next." He opens his eyes giving me that death stare he normally reserves for me when I'm not fast enough to take him out every morning.

"I might just buy the damn tutu myself for her to put on you." He growls my way before turning over to face the other direction.

"Ignore me then. See if I buy you another steak!"

"Titan can have as many steaks as he wants. Isn't that right my big man?" At her voice, he jumps up heading straight to her as she kneels down, kissing his big ass head.

"He's going to lose his street cred if he stays around you for much longer." Her eyes snap to mine for a second before going back to paying attention to the dog.

Titan's eyes seem to roll in the back of his head and I can't blame him for how he's currently feeling.

Hell, if she was rubbing me, my eyes would be stuck at the back of mine.

Putting the potatoes into the skillet with hot olive oil, I place a lid on top and turn back towards the woman that has my balls ready to explode.

"Dinner will be ready soon. Want to find something on that big ass T.V. of yours to watch while we eat?"

"Okay." She shakes her head, walking into the living room, Titan on her heels.

Turning back to the stove, I finish cooking our meal.

A few hours later, we are finishing up a cowboy movie. I've barely paid attention to it.

Between the first and second movie, I lay down on the couch and pulled her back to my front. I couldn't pay attention to the movie if I wanted to. All my blood has settled in my cock and refuses to leave.

As the credits roll, she wiggles against me. An unexpected groan slips through my lips and she goes completely still.

Thinking she'll get up, I wait, not saying anything but when she rolls her hips, her ass once again pushing into my hard as steel cock, I push back into her.

She continues on, doing it again and again until I'm dry humping her curvy ass.

My lips move to the soft skin at the back of her neck. Chill bumps cover her skin at the touch of my beard.

Tired of the limited room on the couch, I get up quickly, swinging her into my arms.

We stare right at each other as I walk us to the bed, laying her down on it.

With my eyes still on hers, my fingertips slide her shirt up, exposing her stomach to my mouth.

My tongue slowly licks a path just above her shorts and the sigh that escapes from her makes me smile.

Raising her slightly to get her shirt the rest of the way off, I throw it to the floor, my eyes glued to her tits that are now exposed to my view.

Crawling over the top of her, I kiss her until she is pushing upward trying to rub herself into me. I stay just out of reach of her. Not only to prolong her pleasure but to keep myself in control.

I haven't felt like I was going to blow my load this early since my high school days.

Moving my mouth down to her nipple, I lick it softly with my tongue then blow on it gently with my breath until she grunts in frustration.

Finally sucking the tip into my mouth, I pull hard, her hands coming up to hold me to her.

"Oh, please." She begs.

Letting go of her nipple with a pop, I move to the other one to give it the same attention.

Instead of letting go though, I continue to suck while one of my hands skims down her stomach, heading into her shorts.

Stopping just above her wet heat, I wait until she is wiggling trying to put herself into my hand before I plunge a finger straight down her center.

My finger glides through her wetness into her. My eyes watching her face as her mouth forms a silent O.

Working my finger in and out of her slowly, I let go of her nipple, kissing down the middle of her body.

With my other hand, I slide her shorts down her legs, exposing her slick pussy to my eyes.

"So fucking wet." I breathe, smelling her husky scent.

Looking up, I see her looking directly at me and I hold her gaze with my own as my tongue comes out, flicking her clit quickly.

Her eyes roll to the back of her head and I plunge my finger into her at the same time as I suck her clit into my mouth, pulling hard.

It only takes a few seconds more before she's screaming out her release.

Getting up, I remove my own clothes quickly, pulling a condom from my wallet and sliding it on before kneeling between her legs once again, kissing my way up her center all the way to her mouth.

Her arms circle my neck at the same time as her legs circle my waist, pulling my cock into her wetness.

I rub in between her folds, coating myself before slowly sinking into her.

Just as I'm halfway in, she jerks me closer with her legs and I plunge all the way inside.

It's fucking torture, painful and the greatest pleasure I've ever felt all rolled into one.

"You okay?" My hand holding her face close to my own.

"Definitely." She whispers with a grin, rolling her hips.

"Oh fuck!" I groan.

She starts to do it again but my hands grab her hips holding her in place. Slowly, I pull nearly completely out before sinking deep into her again, working up to a faster past.

I feel her muscles as the start to clench inside of her, indicating that she is building up for release.

Speeding up my efforts, one hand grabs her head, holding her in a deep kiss as the other pulls one of her thighs up, holding it there allowing me to plunge deeper.

Slamming into her several more times, she screams into my mouth as she goes over the edge and I allow myself to explode into the condom, kissing her the entire time.

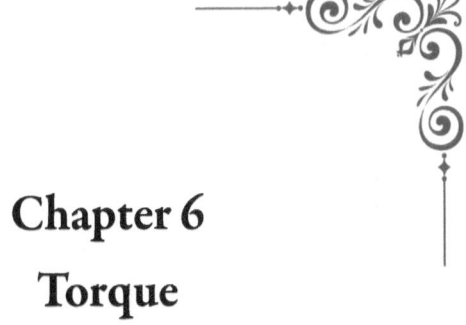

Chapter 6
Torque

Sitting at the table, I listen as the guys all discuss the threat against Jesse as well as the animals.

We left several of the Prospects with her at the clinic while we have this fucked up meeting that's really not getting us anywhere.

"Where's Snake?" I finally ask, noticing for the first time that he's not in the room. If anyone can find some kind of lead, it's that crazy fucker.

"He was waiting on a phone call." Prez answers.

"Since when are we allowed to be late for a fucking call?" Gear, one of the twins demands.

I watch as the Prez's eyes harden, staring straight at Gear until he looks away. The fucker knows better than to question the Prez.

Just as everyone starts up talking once again, the door opens as Snake walks in with his nose still stuck in one of his computers.

Our eyes stay on him, watching as he takes his seat, still not saying a word.

"Snake?" Prez asks loudly.

Snake looks up quickly, surprise in his face like he couldn't remember what room he was in. That's Snake though. He gets lost in data when a computer is around.

"What did you find out?" Prez prods with exasperation.

"Sorry. I started looking into Miss Rayne's family. Especially her sister." He answers and I lean further onto the table.

"Annie Rayne was married quite a few years ago. From the road blocks I came across trying to find this information, someone tried hard to hide that the marriage ever happened."

"Who would want to hide it and why?" I ask before anyone else can.

"My guess is their mom, Charlotte Rayne, she has political connections." He answers.

"Right now I just know she was married. I'm still trying to find out who the guy was, why they divorced and where he is currently. It's the only thing I can find. It's as if the family is squeaky clean." He shrugs.

"No one is that clean." Sprocket, the other twin adds.

"Well at least it's something." Prez sighs. "Torque, ask her about this marriage. Maybe she can shed some light on this. We need to find out quickly if it's a dead-end."

Shaking my head, the Prez dismisses Church quickly so the rest of the guys can get back to the ranch to keep an eye on the horses out there.

Walking out to the bar, I take a seat on the stool signaling to the Prospect to bring me a beer. Bear slaps me on the back as he takes the seat next to me.

"Something tells me you have fallen despite all the negative shit you have spouted over the years about love."

"Nah man, I'm just having fun." I protest even as I feel like I am betraying what Jesse and I currently have.

"I say you're full of shit!"

I sit there quietly not even arguing my case because I have a feeling he's probably right.

"How do you know?" I ask.

"Know what?"

"When you meet the one. How do you know they are the one?" For the first time in a long time I'm being completely honest. He seems to realize that and looks directly at me.

"Honestly?" He waits for me to shake my head. "I knew I was in deep with Sara when I realized that every thought about my future, she was always there. The thought of her not being there scared me more than anything."

We sit there silently after that, just finishing our beers, while I get lost in my thoughts about Jesse.

We've not known each other for a long time but I do look forward to seeing her every day.

Hell, I even like talking to her. That is something completely different for me. I usually like a one and done type deal. With her? I want her even more now that I've had her.

Fucking hell, I am falling for her!

Jesse

"Thank you again! For everything! I just knew I was going to lose him." Mrs. Smith smiles with tears in her eyes as she leaves the clinic.

The poor pup came in with a twisted intestine. It's a rare thing that happens and can be fatal.

I advised her about the risks of it happening again at some point so that she knows to always be on the lookout.

It feels good to work on one that isn't coming in with some kind of poisoning like all the rest. One that really isn't my fault.

With a sigh, I head towards my office when my assistant stops me.

"Your sister Annie keeps calling. As in every ten minutes even though I already told her I would tell you to call her back." Remy says while rolling her eyes dramatically.

"I'll go call her back in my office. Was that the last scheduled appointment for the day?" I ask with hope in my voice.

I'm exhausted from this past week and hoping that things are a little quieter tonight without any emergencies.

Hearing the door to the clinic open, I watch as Torque waltzes inside. His head turning in my direction, he lifts his sunglasses to the top of his head and at the same time I hear Remy gasp. She's apparently noticed those beautiful eyes of his.

Torque however, hasn't noticed anything other than me which is a huge surprise. Remy is tall and slender with gorgeous doe colored eyes.

Yet his eyes never leave my own.

With a smile that is all for me, he takes two steps towards me, wrapping his arms around my waist.

Without a care in the world for whom else is in the room, his lips take mine in a deep kiss that he doesn't let up until I fully kiss him back.

"Now that? Was fucking hot and my cue to go!" Remy laughs, grabbing her things and walking out the door.

"You ready to go?" He asks.

"Absolutely. I need to call my sister back first though." I smile up at him because he still hasn't let me go.

"Before you do that, Prez has some questions he'd like for me to ask you."

"Did you guys find something?" I ask quickly.

"Maybe. We'll know more soon but like I said we have some questions that could help us out."

Shaking my head, I grab his hand pulling him to my office so that we can sit on the small couch that I have there.

Titan is lying next to my desk and raises his head when we walk in.

"I like how I'm now a nobody to you!" Torque growls at Titan and I swear the large beast rolls his eyes before lying back down.

"Fucking traitor." Torque mumbles as I laugh.

"So what are these questions?" I ask expectantly.

"It's mainly about your sister." I look at him with confusion.

"Surely you guys don't think she's behind all this?" I ask.

"No. We are wondering about a marriage that popped up when the club did a background of your sister."

His words catch me by surprise. No one is supposed to know about that. My mom went out of her way to cover the family name over that whole ordeal.

"What about it?" I hedge.

"We found some papers that mention a marriage but we can't find the marriage certificate anywhere or the man's name."

"I'm actually surprised you even found that much." My brain is running like crazy thinking about what Ben did. "It can't be him." I state simply.

"If it can't be then it won't hurt anything for you to tell me his name."

Thinking it over for a minute, I decide that he's right. While no one should know about the marriage, they clearly found something so it's technically not a betrayal to my family.

"Benjamin Brown. You can find him in the California State prison. I put him there."

I watch his eyes take on a surprised look with that last bit of information.

"Why is he in there?" He asks.

"For false imprisonment and animal cruelty." My voice cracks trying to hold the memories at bay.

I don't look up until his hand lifts my chin, holding it until my eyes meet his.

"We'll talk about this more later. I need to go call the Prez, tell him everything you told me."

At my nod, he kisses my lips gently then gets up, striding out the door.

I sit there only a few minutes before walking over to my desk and dialing Annie's number. She picks up on the first ring.

"About time!" She screeches at me.

"I was busy. So why were you calling the office every few minutes and driving my assistant crazy?" I laugh but break off at her words.

"Ben is out." She says quickly.

Feeling like she just pulled the world out from under me, I plop back into my chair heavily.

"How?" Is all I can manage to say.

"He had a parole hearing and they considered him rehabilitated."

"What? That wasn't supposed to be until next month! I got the letter in my desk." I reach into the bottom drawer digging it out to recheck the dates.

"It was supposed to be then but they moved it up for some reason. Mom's lawyer wasn't even made aware of it until this morning after they already released him a couple weeks ago!" The frustration in my sister's voice is very clear.

"Have you heard from him?" I whisper.

"Yes. No. I don't know."

"What do you mean?" I ask with concern.

"I can't be sure that it was him but..."

"But what? What happened Annie?" I almost scream at her.

"The housekeeper let Di outback to go potty over a week ago. When she hadn't returned nearly an hour later, we looked everywhere for her without any luck. We found her today by the back fence. She looked like her neck was broken."

My sister begins to cry over her little dog that she has had for years.

"I'm so sorry Annie. I know how much you loved her."

She cries for a few more minutes before the sniffling stops.

"Look, if it was him, you need to be careful. All I did was divorce him. You made sure he went to prison. Which is what he deserved for what he did to you and those animals."

"I'll be careful. I promise. I'll check back in with you tomorrow. Okay?"

"Love you Jesse."

"Love you too sis."

Hearing Torque at the door, I look up as we both speak at the same time.

"He's out."

"That what your sister was calling you about?" He asks.

"Yep. And to tell me to be careful. Apparently her dog Di went missing over a week ago and turned back up in the yard today with what looks like a broken neck."

"Fuck. It's gotta be him."

Shaking my head, I have to agree.

Torque

As we are getting into my jeep to head home, my phone goes off with a text from Blade.

"Change of plans. We are needed out at the ranch as soon as possible." I throw the jeep into gear and take off down the road.

"What is it?" She asks from the passenger seat.

"It looks like Romeo has been stabbed with something in his front shoulder." I don't tell her the rest. That the other horse that was out in the pasture with him is dead from slashes to his neck.

What kind of a sick fuck would do such a thing? Especially to a horse that could kick or stomp you to death?

I watch as Jesse grabs her medical bag that she always carries with her, digging through it to take inventory of what she has. Anything she doesn't have in that bag we should already have in the fridge that stays in the shed on the side of the barn.

Pulling up to the barn a few minutes later, she jumps out before I completely stop. I narrow my eyes at her but she never even looks my way.

We'll be discussing her putting herself in danger like that. I could have easily run her over with the back tire.

Letting Titan out, we follow her into the barn where everyone else is gathered close to Romeo's stall. Jesse pushes all the leather clad bodies out of her way to get to the horse.

All the guys just smile at her tactics. If they really didn't want to move, she wouldn't have gotten through all of them.

"What pasture?" I ask, watching as she works with the other girls helping her.

"The same one where she fell off his back the other day." Prez murmurs back, staying quiet.

"There's something else?" At my question the Prez indicates for me to follow him outside.

One last glance at Jesse, I walk outside, the rest of the brothers following as well.

"Hayden knows about the other horse being killed but she doesn't know the full extent of the situation." Prez explains, pulling out his phone and handing it to me.

Looking down at the picture on the screen, I see the mutilated body of the other horse and very clearly in its side the fucker carved Jesse's name.

"Fucking hell." I breathe out, handing the phone back to him.

"I'm locking down the club and will expect everyone to take shifts watching the animals. I've also decided that you and Jesse will stay here at the ranch. Hayden and the kids will stay at the clubhouse for now."

"So she's basically bait." I say through clenched teeth.

"We have no idea where this fucker is at. Out here at the ranch there are better spots for the guys to stay hidden so we can see his ass coming. Snake has already gone around hiding small cameras and motion sensors." The Prez tries to make me feel better about it but it's not actually working while I do understand his plan.

At the clubhouse, there is only one way in and only a fool would try that. Out here, he'll think he has a better shot at getting to her or at least he will think he does.

"She better not get fucking hurt!" I stare all my brothers down, one at a time.

I'll make sure of it as I don't plan to let her out of my sight!

Jesse

Finally setting the last stitch, I check Romeo over good to be sure there is nothing else wrong with him.

I've come to love this horse and enjoy riding him every chance that I get. Pisses me off that Ben probably is to blame for this.

"I'm sorry about all of this." I finally say to Hayden who is helping to pick everything up.

"It's not your fault."

"It kind of is. This guy is after me." I finish, looking down at my hands.

"What do you mean?" Bella asks and all the girls turn to me waiting for an answer.

"We think it's my ex brother-in-law. He got out of prison a couple weeks ago and I only just found out today when I talked to my sister."

"I'm going to guess that you had something to do with him going to prison." Mina holds her hand up to stop me from talking.

"Be that as it may, it's still not your fault. You have no control over what another person does. Period." The other girls shake their heads in agreement with her.

"Ladies, your husbands are waiting for you outside." We hear Torque behind us.

I say goodbye to all the girls and Miranda actually hugs my neck before walking away.

Turning towards Torque I notice that his eyes are once again covered by his sunglasses.

"The Prez has put the club on lock down. You and I are going to stay here at the ranch." He says quickly.

"What does that even mean? What's a lock down?"

"Come on. I'll explain on the way to your apartment to get you some clothes." He grabs my hand and I follow willingly.

Chapter 7

Jesse

"We've been here for a week and nothing has happened." I know that I sound like I'm whining but damn it, I'm tired of being here. I'm ready to get back to my regular life!

The only places I've been besides work are here at the clubhouse or the ranch. It's getting old!

"We've got to give him time to settle with your new routine. You changed it up by staying out at the ranch. I'm willing to bet he's watching like a hawk to see where our weaknesses are." Hayden replies from her perch at the bar.

"I just feel like a prisoner. A big fat whiny prisoner." I groan.

"Well, you got one thing wrong there. You're not fat!" I look up to her with a smile.

Everyone in the club is always so nice to me. They are definitely good for my ego. Especially Torque. Holy hell the things that man can do to me.

"Earth to Jesse!" Hayden waves her hand in front of my face. "Where'd you go just then that turned your whole face red?" She laughs knowing exactly what it is without me having to answer at all.

The door opens as Torque and Wrench walk back into the clubhouse. I feel my face flame just from looking at him. Hayden starts laughing all over again causing the men to look at us expectantly.

"What's so funny?" Wrench asks, moving over to his wife for a kiss.

My eyes cut over to Hayden, willing her to keep quiet. Seeing the look I'm throwing at her, she just winks back at me.

"Hey there beautiful." Torque says taking my hand and pulling me to my feet. There is less than an inch of space between our bodies when he looks down into my eyes.

I'm speechless watching his lips move to meet mine. The moment is lost when catcalls and whistling erupt throughout the clubhouse. If I wasn't already red in the face I would probably spontaneously combust right where I stand.

Instead I bury my face in his t-shirt covered chest. He leans down and whispers in my ear, "Wanna get out of here? I've got guard duty in the barn tonight. You could stay out there with me."

Instead of answering him, I nod my head. When he steps away I want to pull him back so I can continue to hide my face, but he takes my hand and leads me to the door.

Just before we step out he calls back over his shoulder, "Ya bunch of jealous pussies."

Getting to his bike he hands me a turquoise helmet I've never seen before. I've been borrowing his and this one is definitely not his.

When I give him a questioning look he just shrugs his shoulders and says, "My woman needs her own."

My eyes cut to his with his declaration of me being his. I guess that makes him mine as well.

Without another word he swings his leg over the bike and starts up the engine. Waiting for me to join him. As soon as my arms reach around him, he hits the gas.

I had been thinking naughty thoughts about him before he even walked into the clubhouse, then the almost kiss and now the bike vibrating between my legs. My brain is being taken over by a cloud of lust.

If we don't get to the ranch quickly I'm going to embarrass myself by coming right here on the back of his bike. An evil thought pops into my head, if I have to suffer so does he.

Wiggling my body closer to him, I lift my legs from the foot pegs and wrap them around his waist. I use the extra leverage to loosen up my arms. Feeling his whole body stiffen, I grin.

In this position it takes me no time at all to get his jeans open. Thank God he goes without boxers most of the time; it makes it easier for me to pull his cock out.

Flying down the road with the wind whipping past us, I stroke him, not caring at the moment if anyone sees us.

So focused on what I'm doing, I don't notice the bike has stopped until he stands up. Lifting me off the bike, charging into the barn.

Torque

I was starting to wonder if Jesse realized the importance of me calling her mine, then she surprised the hell out of me.

Driving down the road while she stroked my cock was a completely new experience for me. Just one look at her bright face proves it's a new experience for her as well.

If I don't get inside her real fast, I'm going to embarrass myself like a teenage boy seeing his first set of naked tits.

As soon as the barn is in sight I park my bike. She is so focused on what she's doing that it takes her by surprise when I wiggle out of her clutches.

Picking her up, I throw her over my shoulder and run to the barn. She smacks my ass a few times but she doesn't really want me to stop.

Climbing the ladder up to the hayloft with her in my arms is tricky but I refuse to let go of her.

Glancing around to make sure we are alone I throw her on the fluffiest pile of hay I can find. Out of the corner of my eye, I see a backpack and some muddy boots but pay it no attention. One of the boys must have forgotten it when we were putting up hay.

Reaching for her waist, I pull her pants and panties off at the same time. I may have never thought of scrubs as being sexy but they sure are easy to remove.

When she reaches for her top, I pull my pants off. Since I didn't take the time to fix myself between the bike and here, they come off quickly.

The whole bike ride was foreplay so I don't waste any time entering her. Sinking right into her wet pussy, I'm in heaven.

With every thrust the word "mine" echoes through my head. When her muscles clamp down on my cock, we both rush over that peak together.

Throwing my jeans back on, I tell Jesse to stay put while I find us something to clean off with. There are towels and running water in the tack room so I head down the ladder. My foot has barely reached the barn floor, when everything goes dark.

Timber

Checking my phone, I see that my message to Torque went through just fine but he has yet to check in.

Walking into the clubhouse I spot Blood standing at the bar talking to his ol' lady and head in his direction.

"Blood! Who else is out at the ranch right now?" I demand.

"Those two new prospects should be stationed in the wooded area facing the barn. Wrench and the other brothers were just headed in through the trail." He answers quickly.

"Hayden should be at the house. She said she needed the reservation book to prepare for the new guests coming in soon." Miranda says from her stool.

"She went by herself?" I demand harshly, causing my brother to give me a look.

I don't mean to sound harsh with any of the women. It just happens to come out that way. Mina has me by the balls and all the women know it so not a damn one of them is afraid of me. As evidenced right now with Miranda grinning at me.

"They thought it would be fine."

"They? Who else is with her?" My heart begins to race.

"Mina." Her one word answer has me fuming mad and anxiety overtaking my entire body like I was just crushed with a ton of bricks.

"I swear to fucking Christ you women are going to be the absolute death of me!" I growl, grabbing my phone from my pocket to call my now missing wife. Her ass had best be okay too or I'm going to burn this place to the fucking ground then whip her ass!

Lucky for her she answers on the first ring.

"What the fuck Mina! Can you women still now follow simple fucking directions?" I grit over the phone.

Glancing back at Blood and Miranda I see that she has that grin still on her fucking face. At my look, Blood whispers to her and she turns away from me.

"We are fine! We are just about to head back. Happy now?" She lowers her voice in that sweet way that she knows gets to me every damn time.

"Yes. I need you to do something for me though before you leave. Go to the barn and see if you can find Torque and Jesse. Neither of them are picking up their phone."

"Okay." She answers.

"Keep me on the phone with you and get your gun ready just in case. The other brothers are headed in but they are probably still a few minutes out."

I listen as she tells Hayden what is going on and gets her gun from her purse, then the crunch of gravel as they head to the barn.

It's completely quiet in the background. Not even the horses are making any sounds.

Signaling to Blood, we head outside towards our bikes. My phone automatically connects to the headset inside my helmet.

"Torque, you guys in here?" She asks loudly as she checks all the stalls. "There's no one here." She says just as I hear Hayden call her name.

"Someone has been in the loft." Hayden says quietly. "Give me the gun. I'll go up."

"Be careful." Mina whispers back.

A few minutes later, Hayden yells to get some help that Torque is bleeding from the head. My tires spin as I take off toward the ranch.

Chapter 8
Timber

"We have every prospect watching every exit out of town but this mother fucker has to be somewhere close by. Snake! Pull up aerial maps surrounding the entire area! We need to see what we have missed." I growl out to the guys just as Doc walks back into the main room.

"How is he?" Blade asks first.

"His vitals all look great at the moment but I'm worried about the swelling at the back of his head." Doc answers.

"When do you think he'll wake up?" I ask, not even considering that he won't.

Doc shrugs slightly, "It's really hard to say. As long as the swelling doesn't get any worse and cause any more damage, all we can do is wait. Someone needs to stay with him at all times for now."

Shaking my head, I look at Bear to see how well he's taking everything. While the two may seem to never get along they are closer than any of the other brothers. Without looking at any of us, Bear turns towards Torque's room.

"Got them!" Snake yells from his computer room and we all head that way.

As he pulls up all the maps across several computers, a migraine starts at my temple.

"Hell, there's too many places to even fucking count! We can't cover all of that!" Wrench says from behind me.

"I agree, we can't." I answer.

"Then what?"

"We know this fuck had easy access to the ranch. His last hit on a horse was in the further back pasture. The same pasture where Jesse fell. We look at everything north of there. Those three buildings." I point to the monitor.

"We'll split up and move in slowly to each one. If the team doesn't find anything, they need to head towards the next closest one to help there if need be." I look at all of my guys who shake their heads in answer. "Once we get to the ranch, we'll use the ATV's but stop far enough away that hopefully this fucker doesn't hear us coming. We ride in ten!"

Giving the order, I walk away to let Mina know what is going on. She and the other girls can keep an eye on Torque.

As I get to the main room, I see her talking with a woman I've never seen before. Slowing my gait, I take in her appearance. No one should have let past the gate so I know this is Mina's doing. Knowing my wife, she did it for good reason.

Finally seeing me walking towards her, Mina motions me forward.

"Timber, this is Jesse's sister Annie. Annie, this is my husband and the President of the club."

When she looks at me, I don't know if the scared look on her face is because of me or if Mina told her about her sister.

"He took her. Didn't he?" She asks, grabbing at a locket she has around her neck.

"We think so."

"God, I wish he had died in prison!" She throws her hands up to her face as she begins to cry.

Mina puts her arm around her trying to comfort her.

"Prez! Torque's awake!" I hear Bear in the hallway. Without waiting to see if Mina gets the crying woman under control I move as fast as I can towards Torque's room.

To see him sitting up is a huge relief. Not only because I was worried about my brother but I'm hoping he has more information that we can go on instead of running out into these damn woods and searching small bits of area.

"Damn! It's good your ass woke up. I thought I was going to have to get Fiona to bring some snakes in here." I grin at the look he shoots me.

"All of you are fuckers!" He groans, feeling the back of his head where he was hit.

"Maybe so but you're one of us fuckers." Bear shrugs.

Looking up to us, Torque asks. "Jesse?"

"We don't know brother." I answer. "We were getting ready to head out on a search until Bear said you had woken. I'm hoping you might remember something that could point us in the right direction."

"I remember we were in the hay loft and I was climbing down the ladder to get a towel from the tack room."

"Do I even want to know why?" He just raises his brow in answer.

"Right before I got to the bottom, I blacked out."

"So you didn't see anything?"

I watch as he thinks it over for a minute, trying to remember all the details.

"There were boots in the loft." He says quickly.

"Boots?" I ask and he shakes his head.

"Yeah. I figured one of the guys left them there.

"They weren't there when you were found so are you sure you saw them?"

"Yes I'm sure! They had red mud caked all over them."

Thinking it over, I move over to the door and call for Snake. I know all the boys are waiting for me in the main room.

"Nice to see you, man!" Snake hisses coming through the door.

"Figures you'd still bring a damn snake in here." Torque says to me.

Ignoring him, I ask Snake to put up the aerial photos around the back pastures once again.

"What are we looking for?" Snake asks.

"The area where the state guys are doing all that digging."

"You mean the area where they think there's an Indian burial ground?" I shake my head at his question.

He makes a few clicks on his computer and right there in front of me is a very clear picture of a huge mound of red dirt.

"Now look North and West of there for abandoned sheds, old home sites or whatever." I demand.

A few minutes later, we've narrowed it all down to just one.

"I'm fucking coming with you!" Torque throws off the covers and starts getting up.

I don't try to stop him. If I was in his shoes and it was Mina, not a damn thing would stop me either.

Torque

Fuck my head feels as though it's been run through a brick wall. The Prez went back into the main room to let the guys know the new plan.

We'll all go in from different positions and hopefully get a direct shot at this crazy fuck before he does something truly stupid that gets Jesse hurt.

I will skin that mother fucker alive if I lose her because of him.

Fucking hell! I've not even had a chance to tell her that I love her yet.

Walking into the main room, I see Mina talking with a woman that looks like my Jesse as well as Jesse's assistant from the clinic.

As I get closer I figure this has to be her sister. The same sister that pissed me off with her messages to Jesse about diets and exercising.

"Torque, this is Annie, Jesse's sister." Mina says as I get closer.

"Nice to finally meet you." I say automatically.

She glances at me for a second before she fully turns in my direction with a huge smile.

There it is. What every woman before Jesse has always done. They are all predictable.

"Well hello." She grins, tossing her hair. "I'm so glad there are so many nice people here willing to help find my sister."

"I'd do anything for the woman that I love." I announce proudly, watching her eyes widen slightly.

"You and my sister?" She asks in a gasp, waiting for me to laugh like it's a joke.

"Absolutely. If you'll excuse me." I smile tightly, walking away quickly.

I wouldn't want to say anything completely out of the way to my future sister in law. It could make my sweet Jesse pissed at me.

Going to the kitchen, I grab something for the pain in my head and down a glass of water before going back into the main room to meet up with my brothers.

"Jesse's sister gave us a recent picture of him." Prez says, holding the picture out to me.

He looks just like any other stupid fuck.

"Not very big, is he?"

"Didn't need to be big to knock you out." Bear laughs when I flip him off.

"Only because he got me from behind." I growl.

"Apparently, Benny boy here has been using Remy for information." Prez says and I look quickly over at Remy who is sitting on a stool with her head down.

"What kind of information?" I growl.

"Jesse's whereabouts, her connection to our club, everything." Blood says quietly.

"Why the fuck would you do that?" I yell at her.

"I didn't know who he was!" She cries out.

"You've lived in this town long enough that you know how shit works here Remy." Prez growls.

"I'm sorry. I'm so sorry." She cries harder but no one moves to comfort her.

Everyone knows the score here. You keep your mouth shut about the club and anyone associated with it.

"We'll deal with her later. Right now, we need to get moving. He's had her for more than half a day. Hopefully she's still alright." Prez says.

"She best be completely alright." I say through gritted teeth.

Pulling my sunglasses over my eyes, I stomp towards the door.

It's time to find my girl and bring her home where she belongs.

Oh, and put a stupid fuck in the ground for worm bait. Can't forget that part.

Jesse

"He'll fucking kill you, ya know." I whisper through dry lips.

"You really think he survived that blow to his head from the shovel?" He laughs. "Highly unlikely."

"If he doesn't, his brothers will kill you."

"I'm not worried about those stupid idiots that try to act all bad because they have big motorcycles. You shouldn't have followed me that day little Jess." He shakes his finger at me. "This is all your fault. Every bit of it. Your fat ass should have died in that hole where I put you."

Remembering that day brings tears to my eyes. When he caught me watching him torture my sisters little dog after arguing with her, he had climbed on top of me and tried to force himself on me.

He got further than I care to admit but my struggling finally landed a blow to his balls and he'd rolled off of me.

I didn't get far before he tripped me, dragging me to an old well and pushed me in.

Stuck in there for several days, I finally was able to climb out. How, I'll never know. But I survived and went straight to the police.

He was arrested within hours and I could finally breathe again. After that, I went off to school and refused to ever go back home.

"I didn't die and I won't die this time. You will though." I whisper.

"Nope. This time I'm going to watch as your life slowly fades from your eyes." He grins, taking a sip of whatever he's drinking from a cold glass.

Just another form of torture from him. He's getting pleasure from it.

I turn my head towards the window to gauge the time. I can only hope that Torque is alright and on his way. If he can figure out which direction we went.

Ben continues drinking as I stare out the window. I don't have any clothes on.

When he grabbed me in the hayloft I hadn't had time to get dressed after my adventure with Torque.

When I close my eyes, I can still feel Torque's hands on my body, the way he fills me so completely. The more I shiver from the cold the more Ben seems to be enjoying himself.

I've been staring out the window trying not to look at him when a sudden noise draws my attention back.

He has moved from the chair and walked to the other side of this one room cabin. That's when I see the cooler.

He reaches in pulling out a bottle of liquor, looking past him I see syringes filled with something packed on one side. Glancing back over his shoulder he sees me looking and pulls one out.

"I bet you wanna know what this is." He says while shaking the syringe back and forth.

I don't respond, this seems to set him off even more. He lunges at me, grabbing my hair, and shoving the needle in front of my face.

"I made some friends in prison. Bet you didn't expect that. Did you know they have a rule in there? It's a simple rule I bet even you would understand. SNITCHES GET STITCHES!!" He screams in my face before finally releasing my hair.

Stepping back he waves the syringe at me one more time. "I thought about using this on you but now I'm going to use it on your boyfriend first. You took my family from me, but maybe I should thank you. If I hadn't shared a cell with Gregory, I wouldn't know about this little combination of chemicals."

He keeps rambling but I tune him out. Something outside has caught my attention. I realize I know where we are. I haven't been to this cabin but I've seen it in the distance from the North Trail.

Returning my focus back to him, he's saying something about making sure my man is dead before he can finish me off.

I watch cautiously as he pulls out a cell phone and sets it on the table. Snapping the lid off the syringe he approaches me.

"I'm going to untie you. You will pick up that phone and call your man. If he answers, tell him to meet you at the entrance to the trails. Don't do anything stupid or I will inject you faster than you can blink."

I realize two things; one he keeps saying 'my man'. That must mean he doesn't know Torque's name, and two I have just seconds to think of some way to give the guys a clue about where I am.

Silently thanking God, Mina made me memorize the club's emergency number; I dial and wait for someone to answer.

As soon as I hear someone pick up, I don't even give them a chance to speak. "Hey this is Jesse. Could you please tell my boyfriend Ridge to leave north at home and meet me at the trailhead? Thank you."

Then I quickly end the call before I lose my nerve. I know there is more than one old cabin out here but if they picked up on my hints at least they'll know the right direction.

Ben grabs my hair again, "What did I tell you?"

"I didn't say anything, I swear." I cry out.

"Who the fuck is north and I thought your man's name was Torque or Tongue or something like that?" He demands.

"His name is Ridge." I insist. "And north is our dog."

He shoves me back into the corner and drops the syringe to tie me up again. For just a moment I think about grabbing the needle but I know I won't reach it before he does.

"You better not be lying to me! Say goodnight." He grunts out before everything goes dark.

Chapter 9
Torque

We all wait for the Prez's command as he takes a call from his phone.

It takes me several long seconds to realize it's the phone used by the club in case of emergencies. Only those directly affiliated to the club have the number.

Prez's eyes connect to mine for a split second before he places the phone back into his pocket.

"It was Jesse." His words cause my stomach to flop.

"How the hell does she even know that number?" I ask.

"Mina made sure she memorized it when she first began working as our veterinarian out at the ranch." Wrench answers.

"What did she say?" I look back at the Prez, waiting.

"She said something about telling her boyfriend, Ridge, to leave north at home and to meet her at the trailhead." He answers.

"She's telling us exactly where she's at." I breathe a small sigh of relief knowing that she's still alive. I won't be able to fully breathe though until I have her back in my arms.

"When we get to the ranch, we'll split up in the ATV's, circling back around to the area she indicated, cutting the motors and walking in so that he doesn't know we are coming." Prez commands loudly so that all the brothers can hear.

"Prez, there's nothing on the maps out that way. I double checked." Snake says.

"Just because we didn't see it doesn't mean it's not. There have been lots of abandoned shelters that we've had to clear as we've bought up the land around here." We all shake our heads in agreement. "Let's go!"

Forty-five minutes later, several of my brothers and I are slowly walking through the trees just north of the ranch, keeping a slow steady pace so as not to be heard.

Signaling to Bear that I'm going further to the right to be farther spaced out, I walk away from my brothers until I can no longer hear the leaves rustling under their feet.

Fifteen minutes later, I can hear the sound of a stream nearby and that is when I catch sight of something further into a thicker copse of trees.

If I had walked up on it from any other direction, I never would have seen it from all the bushes growing so close to the walls, towering over the roof.

There's no wonder why we didn't spot it on the map. It's completely covered up from the brush.

Slowly making my way closer, I get to the nearest tree that I can and that is when the door flies open.

There in the doorway is that fucker and Ben, holding a very naked Jesse with a gun to her head.

"Sneaky sneaky. Tsk tsk!" His grin is almost sinister. "Seen you coming from way back there. You big brutes are all the same. Dumb dumb." He laughs.

"Just let her go man and you can walk away from this." I try to reason.

"Oh no, that would never do. You see, I need her to pay. I'll take everything from her exactly like she did me. Isn't that right you fat bitch?" He says through gritted teeth, reaching up with his other hand squeezing her breast hard enough to make her gasp in pain.

My hand tightens on my gun but I don't have a clear shot from where I'm at. I could accidentally hit Jesse instead. I can only hope that some of my brothers show up before then.

"Don't like when I touch her, hmm?" He asks, keeping eye contact with me as his hand travels further down her body.

Jesse goes completely still, eyes wide with shock. I try to tell her with my eyes to not move until the other brothers get here but just as soon as his finger tips get close to her mound, she begins to fight.

Everything seems to happen all at once after that. I hear a gun go off, blood blasts all over Jesse's face as well as the wall behind them and she begins to scream.

My body is in motion before I have time to think about it, grabbing her into my arms, looking her over in case she was hit.

She buries her face into my shirt as I whisper to her that I've got her now.

I look up towards the trees on the left where the shot came from, expecting the other brothers to come forward.

I see a slight glint, knowing it's a gun, I stand pointing my own in that direction just as Bear, the Prez and all the other brothers break through the trees from the same direction that I just came from.

"Good shot brother." Bear murmurs.

"It wasn't me." I state, still looking to the left.

Seeing my reaction all the other brothers aim in that direction as well.

"Try not to shoot me." We hear in an accented voice. "I'm coming out."

I watch in amazement as Baratta, Fiona's husband and Blood's brother in law steps out from the trees carrying a rifle.

"What the fuck are you doing here man?" Blood growls out as everyone puts their guns away. "Thought you were overseas or some shit."

"I was already headed home when Fi called to let me know what was going on. Figured I'd come in from the highway North of here." He shrugs.

"You know, I've often wondered exactly what it is that you do for a living." Prez says looking down at the corpse at our feet. "Now, I do believe that I don't want to know."

Baratta just smiles at us all. Remembering that Jesse is naked, I slip my shirt off putting it over her head.

None of my brothers have yet to look in her direction and I appreciate that more than they could ever know.

"Blood. You know what to do here. Then torch this place." Prez commands, turning back in the direction in which we came from.

"Torque, Mina and the other girls will meet us back at the ranch. She's probably going to need them." He whispers, finally looking down at her as she tries to burrow further into my chest.

Picking my girl up into my arms, I carry her out of there, not stopping until I have us both in the ATV flying back to the ranch.

Jesse

Torque had to pry my hands loose from his shirt once we got to the ATV that he apparently drove part of the way here on.

He just holds me close, whispering into my hair as we ride back towards Hayden's house.

As the porch comes into view, I spot the girls waiting patiently on the porch. They don't immediately run up; more take their time walking slowly to my side.

"Come on sweetie, let's get you cleaned up." Miranda says softly, touching my hand with hers.

Grabbing on to her, I let them help me from the vehicle and walk me towards the door. My heart starts to race as I get further away from Torque and I cry out, looking back at him.

"It's okay. I'm not going anywhere. Let the girl's help you right now okay? I'll be inside in a few minutes." He smiles at me and I turn back around going inside slowly.

Miranda is the one that helps me in and out of the tub after I feel like I've been in it long enough to get clean.

There was one time where she had to stop me from scrubbing myself so hard in one place. I never even noticed that I was doing it. She gently took my hand, taking the cloth from me and soaped up my back. Never saying a word.

For some reason I feel as though she knows exactly what I'm going through. Perhaps it is something she will share with me one day when I'm finally ready to talk about my own ordeal.

Once in the bedroom, she hands me a shirt that smells suspiciously like Torque and I glance up at her.

"I snatched it from his stuff. Figured it might help. There was a time that I needed Blood's t-shirt that smelled like him as well." She shrugs, turning away from me as I slip it on.

A soft knock at the door has my eyes turning that way quickly.

"It's just Mina. She went to get you something to eat." Miranda smiles, walking over to unlock the door for her.

Again I wonder how she knew that the locked door would make me feel more at ease.

"I brought soup! And a pain reliever from Doctor Ortez. He said that he would be around later to check you over once you are more comfortable." Mina says, sitting everything down on the nightstand.

"I'm not sure if I can eat anything right now." I whisper the first words since arriving on the ATV earlier.

"It's okay. You should take the meds though and try to eat a few bites with them so they don't make you sick." She says.

"Hey." Looking at the door, I see Torque peeping around the corner. "It okay if I come in now?"

"Yes." I whisper quickly.

"Make sure she takes the pain pills Doc sent for her and get her to eat at least a few bites. Otherwise they may make her sick." Mina says, standing up to go.

"We'll check back on you after you've rested. We all plan to stay downstairs for tonight." Miranda smiles, following Mina out the door.

"Take these and we'll see if you can eat a little okay?" Torque moves slowly towards me and it almost pisses me off.

I know why he's doing it. For the same reasons the girls were although them doing so didn't bother me. Just when he does it.

Swallowing the pills quickly, he hands me the cup of soup just as slowly.

"Don't do that." I finally say and he goes completely still.

"Do what?"

"Treat me like a scared rabbit that's ready to run. That's not what I need from you." I state simply.

"What do you need from me?" He takes off his sunglasses looking at me with those amazing eyes of his.

"To be normal." I say a few minutes later.

His beautiful smile stretches over his face making his eyes even brighter.

"I can do that." He answers, stripping down to his boxers and climbing into the bed with me, pulling me into his arms.

I fall asleep wrapped around him as he rubs circles on my back.

Chapter 10

Jesse

"I still jump sometimes at the smallest things. Like yesterday, I was sitting out by the tree reading and I didn't hear Torque walk up until he touched my shoulder. Scared us both with my screaming." I roll my eyes recalling the episode.

"That's normal hon. It'll get less as time passes." Miranda says from her chair at the table.

"It's been months though and I'm so tired of seeing that look he gets in his eyes when he realizes I've been frightened yet again."

I know deep down that Torque still blames himself for not being able to keep me from being taken by Ben in the first place.

He's not to blame. I've even told him so but I don't think he believes me.

"Sweetie, these men go through our trauma with us in their own way. He too, needs time to heal from what happened." Mina explains, popping a strawberry into her mouth.

"I guess you are right." Shaking my head, I go back to rolling out the crust for the pie that I'm making for our

Thanksgiving dinner we are giving to the children at the hospital tomorrow.

"Did you ever manage to get all that pink coloring out of all your clothes?" I smirk over at Fiona who throws me a glare.

"You have to admit that it was a pretty slick prank." Bella throws in, getting a berry thrown at her head by Fiona.

"You bitchs could have warned me about it! You all know I hate fucking pink!" She wrinkles her nose in distaste.

"It still wasn't as great as the snakes Fi. That shit was so funny. I saved the video on my phone. Torque caught me watching it the other day and made me swear that I wouldn't get any crazy ideas from you." I chuckle.

"I still dream of his girlish screams." Fiona closes her eyes with a huge smile on her face. "When are you two going to get married?" She blurts suddenly.

"What?" I laugh.

"You know that ring is coming soon right?" She looks directly at me as do all the other girls with grins on their face.

I look at each one of them for several long seconds before shaking my head.

"No. I don't think it's that far yet."

They all begin to laugh at the same time.

"For an educated woman you sure are a little dense sometimes." Fiona says.

Looking down at the bowl in front of me, I think it over some more wondering if it's what I really want. It only takes a second for me to realize that it certainly is.

Torque

Making sure that I knock on the bathroom door first, I wait for Jesse to tell me to come in.

I hate that small things make her still jump out of her skin. Hopefully with time that will disappear.

Blood talked with me about it quite a bit after what happened even explaining what all him and Miranda went through after she was rescued.

Opening the door, I walk in and see my woman laid back in a bubble bath up to her neck and I chuckle at the sight. Her breasts are too large to be completely covered by the water and bubbles.

"Like what you see?" She finally asks as I've stood there gawking at her.

"Yep." I grin, reaching up to pull my shirt off capturing her attention.

"What are you doing?" She asks huskily and I love that I can affect her that quickly.

"I need a bath too." I keep grinning as my pants hit the floor and my already hard cock springs free.

"Looks more like we are about to make this water dirty." She watches as I walk closer, slipping in behind her.

"Then we'll run more water." I whisper in her ear, picking her ass up and putting her in my lap.

Gliding my cock against her folds. She's already slick from the bath oils she put into the water and sighs as the head rubs her clit.

My hands slide around her body, cupping her breasts and pinching both nipples. Her own hands slide down, touching, grabbing my cock and lining it up.

I slide deep inside of her effortlessly. Her insides gripping my shaft tightly. Gliding in and out of her slowly, enjoying the feel of her until I feel like I'm driving myself crazy.

My hands reach down, grabbing her thighs and pull them up towards her chest and I slide deeper into her working up at a faster, harder pace.

Her hands reach up to grip my neck as I slam harder into her, drawing out every gasp and grunt of pleasure from her lips.

Feeling how close she is to coming all over me, I nip at the base of her neck sending her into spasms that have me screaming at her name as I explode inside of her.

"You're gonna marry me right?" I say a few minutes later once our breathing gets back to normal.

"Is that really your proposal?" She laughs, turning to look at me.

Reaching over the tub to my jeans pocket, I pull out a ring box and open it for her.

"I never thought I would find someone like you. Someone that completed me. And that is exactly what you do. You complete me in every way. I never want to go a day without you in my arms. I love you. Will you marry me?"

I do exactly as Bear told me. Telling her exactly what I am feeling. He said women needed that kind of thing. I'm hoping that he's right.

I watch as she looks at me then at the ring. Her eyes fill with tears and I'm about to jump out of this tub to go kill Bear for giving me shitty ass advice until her words stop me.

"Yes, Torque. I'll marry you. I love you so much!" She throws herself back into my arms, crying into my shoulder.

"So these are happy tears then?" I ask, still unsure if I should shoot Bear.

"Yes." She looks up at me with a giggle, face still wet from crying. "I'm very happy."

"Good." I state, standing up from the bath with her in my arms.

"What are you doing now?" She shrieks.

"Taking my soon to be wife to our bed so I can make love to her properly."

"Oh." She says, wrapping her arms around my neck. "Let's go then."

The End For Now... Continue for a sneak peek at Fang's Miracle, Book 7!

Fang's Miracle

Wolfsbane Ridge
MC

Book 7

Chapter 1

Fang

The clubhouse is busy today with the preparations for Thanksgiving dinner tomorrow at the hospital. Our VP's ole lady started a tradition last year of cooking for the families staying in the children's wing.

"Okay, now that everyone is here, Mina has an announcement to make." Prez speaks loudly to get everyone's attention.

Looking over at his ole lady, I wait to see what is going on. This is obviously not a regular Church meeting because the women are never included in those.

"We are planning to do a secret Santa for the kids at the hospital this year. Tomorrow after all the kids and their families eat dinner, we will each draw names from a bowl. Whoever's name you draw will be who you need to buy gifts for." She looks at the crowd of faces until she stops at mine. "Real gifts Fang."

I smile lopsidedly at her, not saying a word. She already knows me too well. Although I still haven't gotten even with her and the other girls for the frog fiasco a few years back when I was still a prospect. I've gotta admit it was pretty fucking epic what those women planned and executed.

"Don't forget that everyone needs to be on time tomorrow. Those of you that are helping get the food there need to be at Bella's Brew no later than ten a.m. The rest of you should be here to ride to the hospital in formation." Prez says before calling the impromptu meeting to a close.

Walking over to the bar, I spot Dane sitting on a stool with a beer in his hand.

"Getting started kind of early, huh?" I say, taking the seat next to him.

He shrugs his shoulders, "It's five o'clock somewhere."

Signaling to the prospect manning the bar to bring me a cold one, I look back at Dane. He seems to be lost in thought more and more these days.

I've known him for a long time so I know the holidays are a huge problem for him. He's never told me all the details; I just know it has something to do with his family that live back East. Although this year he seems a little worse for wear.

"You okay, man?" I finally break the silence.

"Just been thinking a lot. About family and shit." He looks around the room at the other brothers.

Looking over at the brothers who are married now, some with kids, I too feel a small ache of wanting what they have.

"We'll find what they have one day." I say.

"Fuck. Listen at us. Sounding like emotional ass women." He makes a face.

I laugh, "You started the shit."

"Come on, we gotta go do some manly shit to get our man card back." We stand up, grabbing what's left of our beers, leaving through the front door.

Autumn

Sitting here on the bench outside the hospital, I can't stop the lone tear that slips down my face. I left Dr. Ortez's office about ten minutes ago after he told me that Olivia's cancer is progressing to the point that we need a bone marrow transplant.

That wouldn't be a problem if a donor was easily found but that is not the case. The most likely candidate would be a family member but we don't have anyone except each other. So getting her on the registry and hoping to find a match is the only hope we have.

Drying my face off, I head back inside to Livie's room, hoping she won't be able to tell that I've been crying.

Walking into her room, I see that she is sitting up on her bed playing the video game one of the nurses gave to her when she got admitted last week.

She smiles as I walk into the room. "Hey, mommy, where've you been? You missed all the motorcycles!" She says with huge eyes.

"I heard them. They were loud." I smile at her excitement.

"They were so cool! The nurse says they are friends of Dr. Ortez and that he also rides a motorcycle. Do you think he would take me for a ride?" She's talking so fast, her sentences run together making me laugh.

"Maybe you can ask him later. Before we head down to the cafeteria, I need to talk to you a minute about what Dr. Ortez had to talk to me about." I sit on the edge of her bed with my heart pounding unsure exactly how to tell an eight year old that she needs a transplant.

"We aren't leaving the hospital, are we?" She huffs, lying back against her pillows.

"Not for a while sweetheart. Remember when we talked about what would happen if you needed a donor?" I ask gently.

"I remember. Dr. Ortez said I would have to stay in the hospital for a really long time." She looks at me with so much trust it breaks my heart.

What will I do if we can't find a match in time? How will I explain to my daughter that she could possibly die?

Holding even more tears at bay, I say, "Come on. Let's go eat." I smile standing up next to her bed.

"You think they'll have pie?" She hops up with excitement yet again as if we were not just talking about a longer stay in the hospital.

"Is pie the only thing you want?" I laugh at her.

"Nope. I want some ham with my pie." She nods her head, grabbing my hand as we walk out of the room.

Fang

After helping to set up all the tables with the food, I head outside to a bench that is under a gazebo hoping for a few minutes alone.

Pulling out a pack of smokes, I light one up taking a huge drag, filling my lungs with smoke. The only times I ever smoke are on days that the memories of my baby brother take over my brain.

Being around the kids today at the hospital has brought back memories of him that I try to hide deep inside.

"Those are bad for you, ya know?" A little voice from behind me causes me to jump.

Putting it out, I turn around to see a tiny little girl bundled up in her jacket against the cold wind sitting on the bench I was hoping to pass a little time on.

"I don't do it often." I finally say in reference to the cigarette she caught me with. "What are you doing out here alone?" I look around for her parents but don't see any one.

"Momma is talking with Dr. Ortez again." She rolls her eyes, swinging her legs back and forth.

Looking closely at her, she doesn't look sick but I know that's not an indication that she's not. My little brother didn't look sick either.

"So what's your name munchkin?" I smile when she gives me a look for calling her that.

"Well, it's not Munchkin." She huffs. "My name is Olivia."

Smiling with what I'm about to do, "Olivia is a beautiful name but I think I like Munchkin better."

"Now I know why momma says boys are weird and that I should stay away from them." She shakes her head, never cracking a smile. "What do I call you? Smoke Man?" She says with a grin as I laugh.

"My friends call me Fang." I offer her my hand which she shakes.

"Fang is a weird name. Do you have vampire teeth or something?" She narrows her eyes, looking towards my mouth.

"If I said yes, could we still be friends?" I ask as seriously as I can.

She seems to think about it for a minute before answering. "If you were a vampire and you bit me, would that get rid of my cancer?" Her eyes finally look up into my own and I am struck by the seriousness her dark brown eyes convey.

As I turn her question over in my head, my heart beats harder within my chest knowing that I need to be extremely careful with how I answer her. Right now is not the time for my usual playful nature.

Sitting down next to her, I place my elbows on my knees and look directly back at her.

"I don't know that much about vampire's kiddo but I do know doctors. If there's a way, they will find it."

She looks hard at me for several long minutes as she thinks over what I said before sitting back on the bench.

"I like you Fang." She smiles.

"I like you too, Livie." I respond back with my own grin.

"That's what my mom calls me. Unless she's upset, then she calls me Olivia." She giggles.

"I think Olivia is a beautiful name for a very beautiful little girl." I reach over, putting her tiny hand in my own, giving it a small squeeze.

We sit just like that, lost in our own thoughts for several long minutes until someone else comes out the hospital door.

"Olivia!" We hear her yell, both turning towards her voice.

"Uh oh." Livie and I say at the same time before we start to laugh.

Hopefully the woman coming towards us doesn't plan to eat me alive for hanging out with her little girl.

Autumn

Looking out the glass doors and seeing Livie sitting with some strange man made my throat squeeze up.

Yelling her name as I came out the door didn't seem to faze either one of them because they both broke out into hysterical laughter.

By the time I get to the gazebo where they are both sitting, their laughter has started to fade.

Looking Olivia over first, as is my habit these days, I don't pay the man very much attention.

"It's too cold for you to be out here little lady." I say, kneeling down in front of her.

"I got my coat momma." She giggles. "This is my new friend Fang."

"Fang?" I look over quickly to the man still sitting on the bench.

This close I can see he is a very handsome man, almost too handsome. I realize I've been staring too long when he begins to grin at me and I can feel my face start to flush with embarrassment.

Slightly clearing my throat, I hold my hand out to him.

"I'm Autumn, Olivia's mom. It's nice to meet you." I say, waiting for his hand to shake my own.

I'm not prepared for the electricity that zaps up my arm at first contact with him. I can tell that he felt it too but the slight widening of his eyes.

"Nice to meet you ma'am." He grins again.

Polite and manners, that's rare in most of the men I've met. I think to myself.

"I should get back inside and help my friends." He looks back at the hospital doors before turning back to us.

"Your friends?" I ask, confused.

"Yeah. My club is the one holding the Thanksgiving dinner inside for all the kids. You two should make sure you come in for some food."

He looks over at Olivia directly with another huge grin just for her that causes my heart to beat quickly. No one has ever looked at my daughter in such a way. Most of the men I've tried to date over the years would always see her as a nuisance.

"Is there pie?" Olivia stands up from the bench.

"Absolutely the best pie in the world. One of the ole ladies in the club owns Bella's Brew. Have you ever been there?" He asks her.

Neither of them pays me any mind as they begin walking with each other back towards the hospital doors, chatting the entire way.

I finally pick up my pace, jogging a little to catch up with them.

Fang

Helping Livie fill her plate with all the things she wants to eat, I watch her mother out of the corner of my eye. She seems at a loss for the way that I engage with her daughter.

It's sad to think of what kind of men have caused her to behave in such a way. I couldn't imagine ever treating a child badly. They are the greatest gifts, even if they are not your own.

I lead them both towards a table in the corner, sitting Olivia's food in front of one of the chairs.

We all eat in silence, watching everyone else move around the room talking to each other.

"There's a whole bunch of you. Are they your family?" Olivia asks with awe, scanning the room with her eyes.

Looking around myself, I realize that she is right. There are a lot of us in the club and we all consider each other family.

"We are family because we choose to be family." I answer.

"What do you mean?" Autumn asks.

"When you become part of the club, you swear to put the club family first because we all are more like family than our blood family is. Some of the guys join up simply because they are looking for that family dynamic. It's something they never had with their real families." I shrug my shoulders hoping that I explained it well enough for her to understand.

"So you guys adopted each other?" Olivia asks and I can't stop my smile in her direction.

Only a child could put it so simply but it still hit the mark dead on.

"Exactly."

She grins at me, taking a huge bite of her chocolate pie and I do the same. Both of us are trying hard to not let any fall out of our mouths as we chew.

Autumn

"Fang, are you corrupting one of these kids already?" A beautiful dark haired woman stops next to our table with her hand on her hip.

I feel a slight twinge in my chest at the thought that this woman might be slightly more important to Fang than just family. Perhaps a wife or girlfriend.

"You offend me Mina. I would never do such a thing." He gasps with mock shock, Olivia starts to giggle.

The dark haired woman turns her smile my way.

"Hello, I'm Mina, this big lugs sister." She jerks her thumb his way.

At her admission, the breath I hadn't realized I had been holding let's go of my lungs in time to find my own manners.

"My name is Autumn and that's my daughter Olivia." I smile back at her.

"If he gives you any trouble over here, do not hesitate to let me know and I will send someone to handle him." She tries to say it with a straight face but we all can see the twinkle in her eye.

"Seriously Mina, I'm being an angel today which is more than I can say for Dane, who seems to be about to start a food fight." At Fang's words, Mina gasps, turning towards the commotion in the middle of the room and taking off in that direction.

Fang laughs as he watches her stride up to another man, grabbing him by the ear like a two year old child.

The man in question is just as big as Fang and could easily cast Mina to the side. Instead of doing so though, he seems to be pleading with her to let his ear go.

"He's gonna be feeling that tomorrow." Fang laughs around another bite of pie.

Olivia is also watching the scene across the room with interest, laughing along with Fang.

"She's not afraid of any of you." I say it like a statement although I'm asking a question.

"Why would she be? She's the Queen bee in our club plus we know our manners. Women should never be hurt in any way. Neither should kids." He smiles down at Livie.

She's now looking up at him with eyes that seem to scream that she thinks he's the greatest thing she has ever seen in her short little life.

My heart squeezes tighter inside my chest.

Order Today!
https://books2read.com/FangsMiracle

Sneak Peak

Night Howler's MC
New Orleans
Skeeter
Chapter 1
Katrina

"Ma'am? Can you open your eyes?" I hear from a voice that sounds so far away.

Trying to turn my head in the direction it's coming from, pain shoots through every fiber of my body. A groan escapes my lips, surprising me with the sound.

"Water?" I barely say above a whisper. My throat feels impossibly dry.

I feel cold fingers on my face just as one of my eyes is forced open and a bright light invades the darkness.

I jump, trying to turn away which causes even more pain through my skull.

"Please." I beg, not knowing if these people are trying to hurt me.

"Give her some water!" I hear a growly voice command from somewhere else in the room.

I force my own eyes open, looking for the source of the voice. Everything is fuzzy and blurry.

"Here." I hear the voice yet again but much closer. Almost too close.

I jump slightly feeling yet another touch to the side of my face just before a straw touches my bottom lip.

"Drink. But not too quickly." The voice somehow becomes softer. Forcing my eyes open a little more, I make out the features of the man holding the cup.

Noticing my eyes directed at him, he stares back as I slowly sip at the water.

Letting go of the straw, he pulls the cup away.

"Thank you." I whisper, closing my eyes once more.

"You are welcome, Katrina." He says back but my eyes pop back open.

"Who are you?" I ask.

Smirking slightly, "I'm called Skeeter."

Thinking it over for several long seconds, I reply, "What kind of name is that?"

He only chuckles back in answer.

Looking slowly around the room, I notice what must be a doctor and several nurses in the room.

"Why am I in the hospital?" Looking down at my own arms I realize they are covered in bruises. "Was I in an accident?"

Looking up I see confusion on all their faces. My heart begins to pound at the fact no one is saying anything.

"Can you tell us what your last name is, Miss Katrina?" The doctor asks, moving closer to the bed.

Thinking about his question I realize that I don't remember what it is. I'm actually not certain Katrina is my name either.

"I...um, I'm not sure." Tears invade my eyes. The guy next to the bed puts his hand into mine, barely squeezing my fingers.

"It's okay. There's plenty of time for you to remember everything. For now its best if you rest for a while." The doctor states, writing on the tablet in his hand. "I'll be back to check on you before my shift ends." He smiles, glancing over at Skeeter before walking out the door.

"I should let you rest too." Skeeter says, letting go of my hand.

"You'll come back?" I ask, almost in a panic at the thought of him not being here.

"I won't be far." He smiles back at me before slowly closing the door behind him.

Laying back into my pillow, I struggle to keep my eyes open and realize the nurse must have put something into my IV before leaving with the doctor.

Why can't I remember? I think to myself before falling back to sleep.

Skeeter

"She still doesn't remember anything. Not even her own name. Were you able to at least find a last name for her?" Doc asks outside of Katrina's room.

Watching her through the glass window, I can only shake my head in answer. I come by every day to check on her and to talk with her doctor about her condition.

"Do you think she'll ever regain her memory?" I ask.

"It's hard to say." He shrugs. "The brain is a complex organ that we still don't fully understand."

"It may be best that she doesn't remember. At least whatever part of her life she was in that hell."

"Can't say that I don't agree with you there. I may not know the details but I see her medical charts. She's had broken bones that are healed now but I can tell she never got medical treatment because of how they grew back." He answers. "I have other patients to check on. I'll be back around later before the end of my shift."

"Thank you doctor." I shake his hand before he walks away.

Turning towards her door, I knock gently before pushing it open further.

"Hey you." I greet her with a grin.

"Hey." She answers. The wild eyed look that seems to always be on her face is still present.

"How are you feeling today?" I ask, taking a seat next to the bed.

"I'm okay. The doctor said that I should be able to leave soon." She says softly, looking down at her hands that are twisting the sheet.

"Well that's a good thing right?"

"I guess so." She answers but before I can say anything else her door opens with a nurse coming in.

"Are you ready for your shower?" The nurse asks with a smile.

Katrina looks over at me expectantly.

"Get you a shower. I'll stop back by later." I smile, patting her on the hand and walking out the door.

I have to get back to the clubhouse and make sure my guys got the last set of girls moved into their new homes across the city.

Some of the girls we saved from that warehouse had family that they went back to. But there were still some left that had nowhere to go so the club opened up several of the houses that we had bought in the last year to use as safe houses.

We are even helping them with getting jobs. At least for those who are not so traumatized that they can't work. The ones that needed therapy are getting that as well after I called in a favor.

The feds we were working with are on our asses about where the women are at because only a select few know. I may have allowed our club to work with them but that doesn't mean we trust them. Far from it.

Back at the clubhouse I find Animal, one of the newest club brothers in the main room.

"The women get settled in okay?" I ask him.

"Yeah. Buzz said he'd check in with you later today once he had his sister settled in at his place." He answers.

There's something about Animal that I just haven't ever liked. I've been unable to pinpoint what it is. Something in his eyes maybe that I don't fully trust.

"Thanks. I'll be in my office for a while before I head back to the hospital this afternoon."

"That girl going to be released soon?" His question has me stopping to turn back in his direction.

"There a reason you're asking?" I ask calmly.

Shrugging his shoulders, he says, "Just wondering if she'll need a place at one of the houses."

"I'll let you know." I answer quickly, walking away.

Shutting the door to my office, I pull my phone from my pocket and dial Buzz's number.

"Prez." He answers quickly.

"Thought I'd check in on your sister. How she doing?" I ask.

"She's alright. A little jumpy but I think with time she'll heal."

"She always was a strong one." I smile remembering her younger self.

"Yeah. Did you need something else?" He asks knowing me too well.

"Not really."

He starts laughing in my ear. "I know you man. Talk to me. You have something on your mind that is heavy enough that you called me only to hold the phone like some chick."

"You are an asshole." I growl.

"But I'm an asshole that's right." He laughs again. "So out with it."

"Something about Animal tells me to not trust him."

"He's one of our brothers." He states. "You didn't object when we voted him in."

"It's probably just my imagination." I sigh, rubbing my forehead.

"That is highly unlikely. I'll see what I can dig up." He says.

"Thanks man."

"No problem, Prez." He says as we hang up.

He's right though. Usually when my gut is telling me something is off, it normally is.

Katrina

Looking at myself in the mirror, I don't recognize my face and it's not from all the bruises that are slowly fading away.

I've asked myself numerous times, who are you, only to always come back with the exact same answer. I don't know.

Surely I had a life before this happened to me? Although I can't remember it. I can't even remember what exactly happened to me. Not that anyone has given me the whole story.

Even Skeeter has stayed quiet about some of the details that I know for a fact he knows. He's always so nice about telling me that if I can't remember then it's probably best that no one else tells me either.

Somehow I feel like that isn't the type of person that I am though. I want to know, even if I can't remember it.

The doctor said that I would be released soon but where the hell am I going to go? I can't remember if I have family or not that would take me in.

Sighing heavily I look at myself once more in the mirror.

"I don't know who you are but I am determined to make it." I tell myself with a firm shake of my head.

I'll find somewhere to live and I'll get a job. I'll make a new life, at least until I can remember if I already have one somewhere else.

With a new resolve, I head back to my hospital bed. While I've been getting better, I'm still a little weak in the legs when I've been up too long.

Sighing down into my pillow, I fall asleep wondering if Skeeter will once again be there in the morning when I wake up.

About The Author:

Marissa Ann spends her time in rural North Mississippi with her husband, the kids and all of their animals on a hobby farm.

She always said she would write books one day even though many thought she never would. She made a promise to a childhood friend who left this world for the next in 2015. That she would finally write and publish at least one.

Her first book hit the market in 2018 and she's never looked back. She hit the USA Today's Best Sellers list in December 2021. She now has several out with many more scheduled for release. Want to stay up to date with new releases, giveaways and all the cool things? Sign up for Marissa Ann's Newsletter at **https://www.authormarissaann.com** or join **Marissa Ann Romance Readers**[1] on Facebook.

---

1.   https://www.facebook.com/groups/1543661216008591/